EXODUS: EUROPA

Terence West

EXODUS: EUROPA

A DOUBLE DRAGON PAPERBACK

ISBN 978-1-78695-510-4

Double Dragon
is an imprint of
Fiction4All

This Edition Published 2021
Fiction4All
www.fiction4all.com

Cover art by Deron Douglas
www.derondouglas.ca

CHAPTER ONE

She placed her hands on both sides of the window and pressed her face against the transparasteel. Staring into the inky blackness, she came to a quick realization: if there were life here, it would have to swim up and press its slimy face against the window for her to see it. Or bite her in the ass, but she hoped for the former. Turning away from the window, she wondered why the designers had even decided to install them.

Looking around her cramped quarters, she dropped her bath towel to the floor and snatched a pair of underwear and bra from her bed. Pulling the two articles of clothing on, she grabbed her last clean jumpsuit from a hangar on the wall. Stepping into the suit, she slipped on the arms and zipped up the front to just above her cleavage. Dropping down into a nearby chair, she grabbed a pair of thick, black boots and set them next to her bare feet. Reaching over, she retrieved a pair of socks from the same pile that had held her underwear. Pulling on her socks and boots, she stood and stretched. Glancing at the clock, she decided it was way too early to be awake.

Synchronizing her digital watch to match the clock, she started for the door and stopped. Turning around, she stared at the top drawer of her nightstand. She didn't need it, she told herself. It was nothing more than a crutch at this point. She had been down here for almost a year. The chemical had run its course through her system within the first forty-eight hours of being here. Even the oral fixation had run its course. She no longer found herself chewing on pens or her nails. She had beaten it, yet…there was still something. Cursing under her breath, she quickly crossed the small room and tore open the nightstand drawer. Reaching in, she retrieved a small silver packet and held it in her hand. Shaking her head, she tore it open and removed the small, circular patch. Tearing off the clear backing, she held it up to the light.

"You'd think they would've come up with a better way to quit smoking by now," she laughed uncomfortably. Unzipping her flight suit slightly, she placed the sticky side of the patch on her right shoulder. Taking a deep breath, she began to feel the effects of the nicotine patch. That familiar foul taste was once again in the back of her mouth. Swallowing hard once, she closed her eyes as the first of the medicine began to hit her system. Tossing the spent silver wrapper on her nightstand, she grabbed a black jacket off a wall hanger and headed for the door.

Tapping the panel gently, she waited for the automatic door to slide open. Stepping out into the corridor, she had to squint her eyes. Blinking rapidly, her eyes quickly adjusted to the bright, fluorescent lights. Moving through the halls passed jogging co-workers and the last few members of the night crew, she found herself in the mess hall. Taking a deep whiff of the air, she could smell freshly brewed coffee. Moving quickly to the bank of coffee pots on the far side of the room, she grabbed a cup and poured the thick, black liquid into it. Lifting it to her nose, she inhaled deeply and sighed with pleasure. Lifting the cup to her lips, she took a long drink. She could quickly feel the warmth spread down her esophagus to her stomach. The taste of the coffee almost overpowered the horrid taste the nicotine patch was creating…almost.

"Dr. Sumner, please report to decon. Dr. Sumner, please report to decon. STAT."

Dr. Julie Sumner stared up at the speaker built into ceiling in awe. She wasn't even on duty for another forty minutes and they were already paging her. Taking another drink from the coffee cup, she set it on the counter. Tossing her wavy brown hair over her shoulder, she moved into the hallway and headed for decon. Taking a quick left, she skidded to a stop in front of the elevator. Hitting the call button impatiently, she waited for the familiar ding to announce the lift's arrival.

"Julie!"

Julie turned to see her colleague, Dr. Jim Marcus, charging toward her. Coffee cup in one hand, datapad in the other, he looked as if he had just rolled out of bed. In fact, she could still see a mark from his pillow on his left cheek. His blue jumpsuit wasn't zipped up past his midsection and his black jacket hung off his left arm. "What's the rush, Jim?"

"What the hell is going on this morning?" Jim flipped his head and tried to toss his thick, black dreadlocks out of his face. His face was cleanly shaven, except for the thick tuft of hair he had been cultivating on his chin for the past few months. His gold-rimmed glasses looked good against his dark skin. He was the smartest person here, next to Julie, of course.

"What are you talking about?" Julie asked incredulously. "I just woke up and was paged."

"You haven't heard?"

Julie tried to feign interest in the conversation, but was failing fast. She just wished the damned elevator would arrive. "No, what?"

"The research team," Jim said quickly, "they apparently found some seriously weird shit this morning."

Julie's interest suddenly skyrocketed. "What did they find?"

"I don't know," Jim said excitedly as he swallowed a gulp of coffee. "The buzz down in the archaeology department is palpable, though."

"How did you find out?"

Jim smiled. "I have connections. I don't stay in my quarters reading reports all night. I actually go out and meet people."

Julie rolled her eyes at the not so cleverly veiled knock at her.

"I got a wakeup call from Dr. Rasmussen. He said the research team uncovered," Jim searched for the word, "something."

"Something?" Julie echoed. "Can you be a little more specific?"

"No," Jim admitted. "I don't have all the details, but I will if you let me tag along."

A quizzical look once again appeared on Julie's face.

"You were just paged to the decon area," Jim said quickly. "That's where the research team that found whatever the hell it was is."

Julie furrowed her brow. "Why are they calling me? I'm the station's psychologist."

Jim shrugged. "I don't have clue one. But I do know they'll need a good biologist."

“And of course, you volunteer,” Julie said as the elevator finally arrived. Stepping inside, she turned and looked at Jim. “All right, come on.”

Jim smiled as he bounded into the lift.

“If anyone asks,” Julie said as the elevator doors began to slide shut, “you coerced me.”

Jim nodded. “Fair enough.”

Reaching over, Julie tapped the lowest button on the elevator and felt it whir to life. Leaning back, she crossed her arms in front of her chest. “Still dating that girl in cryonics?”

Jim shook his head with a laugh. “Nah. She was a little weird.”

“What happened?” Julie asked, careful to keep an eye on the descending number above the doors.

“She started talking about freezing rats, or something like that.” Jim laughed.

“She’s in cryonics,” Julie argued, “that’s what she does!”

“I know,” Jim smiled, “but she started to give me the heebie-jeebies.”

“You’re such a jackass.” Julie laughed for the first time. “What are you going to do if you run into her on the station? This place is big, but not that big.”

“We’re cool. I told her I was being transferred to Neptune Station in three weeks.”

“And what if she sees you here after that?”

“I’ll just tell her that my transfer fell through.” Jim adjusted his glasses, “and that I’m gay.”

“Very tactful.”

“I thought so.”

Glancing up at the digital readout, Julie noted they were two floors away from their destination.

As the doors chimed and slid open, all hell broke loose.

Three nurses ran furiously across the room as shrieks of pain and terror filled the air. Four men, still partially in their bronze-colored environmental suits writhed on the floor in agony. The closest man, one of the head archaeologists on the station, was tearing at his eyes with his fingernails. Streaks of blood ran down his cheeks from his eye sockets as he continued to scratch and tear at them. As the nurses tried to tend the men, one looked up and spotted Jim and Julie standing slack-jawed in the elevator.

"Dr. Sumner?"

Julie nodded hesitantly.

"Dr. Sumner, we need you!"

Julie shook her head. "I'm a psychiatrist!"

"But you are a doctor!" the nurse argued as she tried to pull the archaeologist's hands from his bloody eyes. "Please!"

Jim placed his hand on Julie's shoulder and stepped forward. "I'm a doctor, too." Grabbing Julie by the hand, he pulled her into the decon room just as the elevator doors slid shut behind them. Dropping down to his knees next to the nurse and archaeologist, Jim stared in awe at the man. "What the hell happened here?"

"They were coming back in and getting ready for decontamination procedures," the nurse reported quickly. "They all seemed fine, then they just went crazy."

"I need twenty ccs Thorazine," Jim said quickly. Grabbing the man's hands from the nurse, he nodded. "Go." He turned and looked at Julie. "I need some help!"

Julie swallowed hard and dropped down next to Jim. Pulling a small flashlight out of her jumpsuit pocket, she leaned close to the archaeologist. Placing her hand gently on his forehead, she shined the light directly into his eyes and quickly pulled it away. "Pupils are nonresponsive," she breathed. "He could be having a seizure or psychotic episode."

The archaeologist's back suddenly arched and he twisted into a painful position. His eyes snapped shut as blood began to pour out of his eyes, nose and ears. Contorting his body, the man screamed at the top of his lungs. Jim glanced up to see the nurse standing above them with a syringe in her hand.

Quickly grabbing it from her, Jim popped off the top with his thumb and turned it over.

"Hold him!" he shouted.

Julie and the nurse leaned in and grabbed the man's arms and torso. Pressing him flat to the ground, they struggled to hold him still. Tearing away a piece of the environmental suit over his shoulder, Jim jabbed the needle into the newly exposed flesh and quickly emptied all the medicine into the man. Julie felt his convulsions lessening as the Thorazine quickly went to work in his body. As he took a deep breath, his head fell back against the floor.

Pressing her fingers to the soft flesh of his throat, the nurse checked his pulse. "He seems to be coming out of it."

The room suddenly went quiet.

Jim and Julie looked up to see the other men lying perfectly still. The other nurses stood motionless over them, unsure of what had happened, or what to do next. Dropping the spent syringe on the floor, Jim stood and took a full step back from the research team. Julie was next up.

Grabbing the nearest nurse by the arm, Julie lifted the woman to her feet. “Why was I called down here?”

“You were the first doctor on today’s call sheet,” the nurse confessed. “I didn’t know you weren’t a doctor. I didn’t know what to do.”

“Where’s the attending physician?” Julie asked angrily.

The nurse covered her mouth and pointed to the corner of the room nearest the entrance to the wet lab. Jim and Julie turned to see a man wearing a blue jumpsuit and white lab coat twisted unnaturally in the corner. A single trickle of blood ran down from his mouth.

“My God,” Julie gasped, “what the hell is going on here?”

“As the men cleared decon,” the nurse breathed, “they started to enter this room. When they started to freak out, the doctor tried to restrain them. One of the research team threw him back toward the wet lab. His neck was snapped by the decon door as it closed.”

“Jesus,” Julie said under her breath. “What the hell happened to these men to cause them to go crazy like this?”

“We need to get them to the med bay now,” Jim commanded. “Get a HAZMAT team down here ASAP. In the meantime, no one leaves this room.” The lead nurse quickly stood and began to carry out Jim’s orders. “What are you doing?” Julie asked.

“These men could have been exposed to something,” Jim replied, “and that means everyone in this room has been as well.” He looked nervously at the four men lying unconscious on the floor. Moving back against the wall, he slowly sank down to the floor. Tapping a sequence of buttons on his wristcomm, he looked up apologetically to Julie. "We have to institute quarantine procedures."

"Sir?"

***

President Richard D. Wilson looked up from his desk. Pulling off his glasses, he tried to scoop his paperwork into a single pile. "Come on in, George."

George Rosenbaum, a portly man in his fifties, was the President's Chief of Staff. He stood just inside the door of the President's office. He wore a light gray suit with a wrinkled red tie. That was a bad sign. George Rosenbaum was never disorganized. "Mr. President," he took a long breath and decided to drop the formality. "Rick, we have a problem."

"What is it?" the President asked, genuinely concerned.

"We've just received word from Europa Station," George said as he took a step into the President's office. Closing the door behind him, he quickly traversed the United Earth seal on the floor. Placing his hands on the President's desk, he leaned over and lowered his voice, "There has been an incident."

"Jesus, George," the President spat out, "just tell me."

"This news is three hours old," George looked his old friend in the eyes, "four people are dead."

"What the hell? Who?"

"Three researchers and a doctor."

The President sat back in his padded leather chair and began to rub the gray hairs in his beard. "What happened?"

"We honestly don't know," George said apologetically. "All we've received are fragments of information. We do know that Europa Station is going into lockdown. Nothing in, nothing out."

"Absolutely not." The President slammed his fist against this desk. "I can't have the biggest research station in the solar system shutting down. That would be catastrophic to the fleet."

"I don't think you understand, Rick." George realized the tone he had taken with the President and quickly rethought his strategy. "We could have some kind of virus down there, some kind of contamination. If that spreads throughout the fleet, we're looking at a mass epidemic. That would probably end your political career real quick."

The President glared at his Chief of Staff. He hated being threatened. "What the hell do you want me to do, George?"

Reaching into his pocket, George produced a small disk. Placing it into the viewer on the President's desk, he scrolled through the directory until he reached the desired file. Accessing the image, he pressed a single button on the base of the viewer that transferred the image to the wall viewer. "The research team found this just before they returned to Europa Station."

The President slowly stood from his chair. "My God." Walking across the room, he placed his hand on the image and traced the clearly defined lines with his fingers. "This is," he paused, "incredible." Taking a step back from the viewer, he tried to take in the ramifications of what he was looking at. It seemed almost unfathomable. "After all these years there…" He tried placing his hands on his hips, but couldn't find a comfortable position. He simply let his arms hang limp at his sides. "Who else has seen this?"

"Only myself and those who transmitted it from Europa Station," George answered. "It was received on a secure frequency with instructions 'for your eyes only'."

"This is the answer man has been looking for since," the President took a moment, "since time began."

"I know."

"What the hell am I supposed to do with this?"

George looked at the image again and smiled. "Provide the answer." He reached over and patted his friend on the back. "Your approval rating will go through the roof."

The President smiled. Turning back to the screen, he took another long look. Amidst the darkness of the photo, he could clearly see a column with some sort of writing on it washed in green light. It seemed vaguely familiar, but completely alien at the same time. This was obviously taken beneath the water on Europa. He could see small particles floating captured by the flash of the camera. Letting his eyes wander down to the base of the column, he made out a partial face staring out of the mud and silt that comprised the bottom of the Europan ocean. It seemed to be part of an ancient statue long since crumbled to the ocean bed. It had human features, but it obviously wasn't. Running back to his desk, he pulled the disk from the viewer and handed it back to George.

"I want our best techs on this right now, and I want it classified above P- One. We need to be damn sure this isn't a hoax, natural rock formation, or some trick of the light like that damned face on Mars turned out to be."

George nodded and stuffed the disk back into his pocket.

The President reached over and tapped a single button on his phone. "Miss Johnson?"

"Yes, Mr. President?" a friendly female voice replied over the intercom. "Get me the Vice President now."

CHAPTER TWO

The Jovian system loomed large in the view screen. The mighty storms of the fifth planet of the solar system swirled endlessly. The big red spot, which was the solar system's oldest storm, seemed to watch their approach as it churned through the lighter layers of clouds around it. The four Galilean moons appeared as little more than dark spots on Jupiter's surface at this distance, but were still impressive. At this point, well over one hundred and twenty moons had been discovered in the system, but only the four originally discovered by Galileo in 1610 captivated people's minds.

Staring out through the view screen, he couldn't help but be in awe at the sight. Jupiter was immense. The bands of yellow, red and orange clouds that encircled the planet spun at different speeds as they moved over the behemoth's surface. He wondered for a moment what they hid beneath them. No probe, even with all their current technology, had been able to survive the plunge into Jupiter's atmosphere. The closest they had come had been one aptly named the "Jupiter Explorer". It had descended into the thick layer of clouds and had been able to take readings, but had been caught in a fierce electrical storm nearly halfway to its final destination. The Jupiter Explorer was struck down by lightning, fiercer than anything experienced on Earth. Not quite the result they had been looking for, but at least they knew there was a small, solid core beneath the clouds.

Moving his hands from the arms of his chair, he ran his fingertips lightly over the console in front of him. The brightly lit buttons and panels displayed information vital to his station and the ship in general. Keying in a specific sequence of instructions, the view screen shifted to Jupiter's four largest moons. Two of them in particular, Io and Europa, held special interest. During the flybys of the Galileo probe at the beginning of the twenty-first century, the two moons had piqued researchers' interest. Io was found to be the most volcanically active body in the entire solar system, but an even more interesting find was housed beneath Europa's icy shell: a liquid ocean. It was the only place known in the entire universe where an ocean occurred besides Earth. Most scientists theorized it could contain more water than all Earth's oceans, seas and rivers combined.

It was also his destination. Early in the 2300s, a permanent colony was built on Europa deep beneath the ice. It was a technological marvel the engineers at the United Earth Space Agency had touted as "the first step into the rest of the galaxy". Ever since 2297 when water became the key component used in starship engines, Europa had gone from a curiosity to a full-fledged interstellar depot.

"What's our status, Captain?"

Captain Alexander Hull spun in his seat to see the visitor who had just entered his bridge. As the doors slid shut behind him, his white uniform shone in the bright lights. "On schedule," Hull assured him. "We'll be arriving at Europa Prime in less than ten minutes."

"Good," Jackson Wyman nodded. Wyman had just been named Vice President of the United Earth government. Holding the rank of admiral and previously the head of the Ministry of Defense, it had been quite a coup when the President announced his name at the previous week's press conference. Next in line for the position had been the head chair of the Senate, but he'd been unceremoniously passed up. In his mid-fifties, Wyman's years in the MOD had softened him. No longer the rough, rugged Commander of Naval Operations that appeared in children's history lessons for winning the battles of Hawaii and Cydonia, he had grown portly over the years. Hull knew it was because he was sitting behind a console instead of being on the front line with his troops. Gone was the look of determination he had seen in photos and vidclips, now Wyman just looked worn and tired. Space had that effect on people. The low gravity, natural radiation, and travel times could make anyone look tired.

Hull was in his third tour of duty as captain of the UESA Tereshkova, named for the first woman cosmonaut launched into space in 1963. He was a well-worn spacer, having logged over fifteen years flight time, making him second to very few in the UESA in total time in space and successful missions. Hull's accomplishments could fill almost as many volumes as Wyman's, but he preferred not to rest on them. He was content to hold the rank of captain and continue runs from Earth to Neptune Station. It wasn't the most glamorous route, but it was what he wanted. No longer concerned with climbing up the ladder of success, Hull was happy ferrying supplies back and forth between the colonies. Or at least he tried to convince himself of that.

In his early forties, Hull's eyes seemed slightly dulled. Not out of shape, but his body was nonetheless starting to gain in girth the longer he sat in the captain's chair. His usually short-cropped hair was starting to become a bit ragged, while his usual five o'clock shadow was beginning to look more like a full-fledged beard. His dirty, dark blue jumpsuit had also seen better days. The black jacket he wore bore his name, rank and circular mission patch on the shoulder. The patch, bearing an image of the Russian space capsule, Vostok 6, orbiting the Earth with Sol burning brightly in the distance, was torn down the center from an engineering accident a few days back. He had intended to replace it, but just hadn't had the time, or the drive.

"You might want to take your seat, Mr. Vice President," Hull said as several warning lights began to blink on his console. "We'll be shutting down artificial gravity in a few moments so we can dock."

Wyman nodded. "Thank you, Captain." Turning, he hit the access panel next to the door with his palm. With a hiss, it slid open revealing the immense hall that ran the entire length of the Tereshkova. Stepping outside, the Vice President moved to the left of the hall and climbed into the waiting transit car. Strapping the restraining bars over his chest, he leaned over and punched his destination into the keypad in the center of the vehicle. The transit car, an eight-seat vehicle used to quickly traverse the length of the ship, was situated on two rails slightly raised from the floor. Utilizing restraining bars and inertia to keep passengers seated, the transit car could be operated in normal or zero gravity conditions. Wyman likened it to the ancient roller coasters he read about in history books. Why anyone would voluntarily choose to ride anything like this was beyond him. He hated the damned contraption. It always made him sick to his stomach. Tapping the activation key, he felt the vehicle shudder to life. Moving forward slowly, it quickly accelerated and was gone.

Hull, standing silently in the bridge's entrance, chuckled to himself as Wyman's scream faded into the distance. He never got tired of that. Turning, he headed back to his station. Glancing across the long, rectangular bridge, he noted the four empty terminals situated below his centrally located seat. Two lowered rows housed the four stations, placing the tops of the chairs at Hull's feet. This gave him an unrestricted view of the main screen taking up the entire front of the bridge and wrapped about a quarter of the way up both sides. A long catwalk ran down the center of the bridge with ladders heading down into "the trenches", as they had come to be known. The bridge was relatively Spartan in design. Hull assumed the designers had done so to keep the command crew's mind on task. Everything they needed was at their fingertips.

The UESA Tereshkova, a Victory class ship, was nearly fifteen hundred meters long and predominantly cylindrical. Engines, fuel storage and cargo space composed nearly three-quarters of the ship. All command and personnel areas were relegated to the remaining quarter. A spherical command center was situated in the front, making it resemble a thermometer. Midway between the command pod and the eight cylindrical engines arranged in two horizontal rows, were the main living quarters. The area was designed with expansion in mind as each was installed as a removable pod. The pods fit end-to-end like building blocks and stretched out from the central cylinder like a large cross. A circular restraining wall attached to the end of each arm connected the compartments via another transit car. Currently set at the bare minimum of pods, the crew quarters revolved slowly creating artificial gravity for the rest of the ship. Finally, behind the crew quarters was a large rectangular bulge that held the cargo area.

There were nineteen other Victory class vessels in the UESA fleet. They had been in service for close to twenty years and had at one time, been the crowning jewel of the fleet, now they were little more than the workhorses. The faster and more streamlined Triumph class now handled more passenger and military duty. Tereshkova had required a computer overhaul to even communicate with Europa Prime Station during their last visit to Earth.

That's what confused Hull about the Vice President's visit to Europa: why was he aboard the Tereshkova when he could have taken one of the Triumph class ships? It seemed to Hull something was slightly amiss on this trip. Wyman's trip had, so far, been kept very quiet as opposed to the usual fanfare related to a major politico visiting one of the outer colonies. Security had been doubled aboard the ship. It seemed a little strange, but Hull had seen stranger.

He let it drift from his mind. It wasn't his concern. They would be entering the Jovian radiation belt in a few moments and docking with Europa Prime. He had to make preparations. Sliding into his chair, he pulled the console across his legs and snapped it in place. Tapping a red button on the far right of his controls with his thumb, he heard a familiar attention whistle across the intraship intercom.

"Attention, this is the captain," he said slowly, listening to his voice echo through the ship. "We'll be shutting down artificial gravity in two minutes. All senior staff to their stations."

Lifting a small, black object from his console, he fitted it in his right ear and adjusted the long, thin mic arm that hung down from it. Once he was comfortable, his fingers flew across the console. "Europa Prime," he said into the mic, "this is the UESA Tereshkova. Do you copy?"

"We have you on our screens now, Tereshkova," a friendly female voice replied without a hint of static. "We have your ETA at five minutes and thirty-three seconds."

Hull double-checked the readout on his panel. "Confirmed, Europa Prime." He tapped the mic again, "Europa," he paused, "are you aware of our cargo?"

"Acknowledged, Tereshkova," the female voice replied again. "We have already made preparations for its arrival."

Hull was unsure why he had inquired. "Thanks, Europa Prime. We'll check in once we're through the radiation belt."

"Have a safe flight, Tereshkova," the perky voice replied.

"Thanks, Europa Prime."

"We'll see you on the other side. Europa Prime out."

Hull popped the mic from his ear just as the door behind him slid open. The rest of his bridge crew quickly flooded into the room and down into the trenches. Strapping themselves in, they began to quickly run over a series of diagnostics. This would be the first time since the upgrade they had docked at Europa Prime. Even though the numerous simulations they had been through had all been successful, they knew in the real world, anything could happen.

Hull tapped a few keys and quickly punched in his security code linking all the bridge consoles to his. He now had a visual readout of everything happening on all consoles right in front of him. Some of his bridge crew argued it was redundant for him to watch every keystroke they logged, but he needed all the information available to make a split-second decision if necessary. The commands on his console started to roll in as each of the four stations went live. Hull nodded in approval as each of his bridge crew remembered their new training. They had a little less than four months to familiarize themselves with the new controls and computer commands, but were performing well. The computer was smart enough to handle a few operator mistakes and correct for them, but if bad commands started to pile up, it could be catastrophic.

Hull glanced at the first station to his left. “Science?”

“Acknowledged,” a young man with jet black hair replied, “and on-line.” He was Ensign Jorg Jansen, a relatively new recruit to the Tereshkova. UESA had assigned him during their last refit on Earth. It seemed Jansen was well thought of by the powers that be. New recruits were often assigned to station duty before taking on space missions to get their “space legs”. Jansen had bypassed an entire area of standard training and been assigned the fifth seat, well ahead of more deserving candidates Hull noted. Still, two weeks into the mission and Jansen had been nothing short of perfection in his duties.

Hull turned to his right. "Engineering?"

"I'm here, dammit," a gruff voice replied. "Anyone else notice this friggin' computer has an attitude?"

Hull would have laughed out loud if they weren't just about to enter the Jovian radiation belt. He quickly cleared his throat and looked accusingly at the engineer. He had come up through the academy with this man. His outward appearance betrayed his actual age. He wasn't much older than Hull. "Engineering?" he asked again, more sternly.

"Acknowledged," the grizzled man said, "and on-line." Chief Engineer Christian "Chris" Beck was probably the best damned engineer in the entire fleet. He could fix an engine with little more than gum and a shoestring if he had to. Oil, grease, or any other substance he could find to rub through it usually darkened his snow-white hair. Wearing the same blue jumpsuit as the rest of the crew, he had orange stripes around the sleeves signifying he was part of the engineering core. His station was always littered with tools, blackened rags and the odd candy wrapper. If he were to ask Chris any technical question related in some way to space travel, he would receive an almost instantaneous response. If he took Chris to a high-class dinner, Hull would find Chris hiding under the tables by the end of the night. Hull understood that Chris was brilliant, and by proxy, that made him socially retarded.

"Navigation?" Hull asked.

"Acknowledged," the third seat replied, "and on-line." Hull leaned over slightly to make sure there was someone actually sitting at the navigation console. He knew better, but it was just that Lieutenant Katrina Cody was a very quiet woman. How she had ended up in the third seat was still beyond him. It was probably due to skill alone. She had very little in the way of social graces or, Hull cringed, a personality. She was all about the job. Most of the time, that suited him fine, but occasionally, he wanted to know a bit more about his navigator. Cody was just a hair over five feet tall with shoulder length brown hair.

She was thin enough that sometimes, Chris asked her to climb into tight spots for repairs others couldn't get to without dismantling the entire wall.

Hull turned and looked at the second seat. "Tactical?"

A young blonde woman turned and looked back at Hull from her position in the forward tactical station. "Acknowledged," she said quickly with a heavy Russian accent, "and on-line." Commander India Kira was Hull's second-in- command. She was next in line for the captain's chair if Hull stepped down or took a different assignment. She had served dutifully under Hull for nearly eight years now, and he could hardly imagine anyone else sitting in the second seat. Kira was stunningly beautiful as well. She could have any man she wanted, but her job was her life. Crewmembers often described her personality as "cold" or "icy". It wasn't because she didn't care, but if the conversation didn't have anything to do with work, she wasn't interested.

Hull leaned back in the first seat and tapped several commands into his panel. Such was the life of a spacer. He spent months at a time in deep space with only his crew to keep him sane. These people become his brothers, sisters, and sometimes, children. This job, unlike any other, had personalities to deal with. At a regular job, he could easily fire someone, or just send him/her home if they weren't "playing nice". Here, by comparison, the only solution was to make the best of it and work around the offending personality. It was part of being captain. He was required to be part leader, part babysitter and part engineer.

"Five," Hull said, referring to the science station's designated number, "Time to radiation belt?"

"Twenty-two seconds," Jansen replied.

"Four," Hull turned his attention, "shut down artificial gravity."

"On it," Chris replied. "Stopping rotation and preparing to lockdown crew and science quarters." A klaxon started to blare through the ship.

"Kill that damned alarm on the bridge," Hull snapped. Reaching over his shoulder, he pulled two harnesses across his chest and locked them into the buckles between his legs.

"Sorry, Skipper," Chris replied as his fingers flew quickly over the keyboard. "We haven't got the computer programmed correctly yet. Still some of the factory presets in there." The alarm was instantly muted on the bridge, but it could still be heard echoing throughout the rest of the ship. "Outer ring is locked down," Chris confirmed after a moment. Pulling his own harnesses across his chest, he began to feel weightless. Grabbing his greasy rags off the deck as they began to float into the air, he quickly stowed them in a small compartment just beneath his console.

"Two, how's the weather?"

Kira turned and looked over her shoulder, her harnesses holding her in place. "Smooth sailing ahead, Captain. Path is clear." Digging into one of the many pockets of her flight suit, she pulled a rubber band out and quickly put her hair into a ponytail. It kept it from floating freely in all directions and inadvertently obscuring her view of the panel.

Hull nodded and smiled. "Three," he said slowly as he stared at his console, "we're slightly off trajectory."

"Correcting," Cody answered. "Ship's drifting a bit." Hull turned to Chris.

"Checking," he said without even looking at Hull. "Seems engine number four is burning a little cooler. Can't correct in flight. Will have to do a complete diagnostic when we dock at Europa Prime." He tapped several more keys on his panel. "I'm adjusting the other engines to match."

Hull nodded. "Three, you better recompute."

"Recomputing now, Captain."

"Six seconds to radiation belt," Jansen announced. "Deflector screens to full," Hull commanded.

As the Tereshkova hit the edge of Jupiter's radiation belt, it shuddered slightly. In the view screen ahead, a myriad of colors blotted out the view of Jupiter and its moons. Hull never tired of this view. From reds, greens, blues and yellows, it was better than watching the Aurora Borealis back home on Earth.

The intense colors were a by-product of the natural radiation from Jupiter interacting with the Tereshkova's electromagnetic shields. Once inside it, the shield harmonics would be tuned to exactly match those of the belt canceling out the colors, but for a moment, they were beautiful. Hull smiled. They were lucky to have the shields. If not, travel to Jupiter and Europa would be impossible. The amount of radiation in the Jovian system was enough to kill a man in less than ten minutes. Only deep under the thick ice of Europa were they safe from it. As the colors on the view screen quickly faded, Hull returned his attention to the task at hand.

"ETA to Europa Prime?"

Cody transferred a plotted trajectory to his console. "Just under four minutes. We're passing through Ganymede's orbit right now."

Hull lifted the small mic from his console and placed it back in his ear. "Europa Prime, this is Tereshkova," he said, keying the mic. "Europa Prime, this is Tereshkova. Do you copy?" The slight hiss of static filled his ear. "This is Tereshkova, do you copy, Europa Prime?"

"We have you, Tereshkova," the perky female voice replied after a long moment. "You just appeared on our scopes again. How was the ride?"

"Beautiful, Europa Prime."

"Acknowledged," the woman said knowingly. "Begin docking sequence at your convenience."

Hull smiled. "Confirmed."

Ahead, he could see Europa looming against the orange surface of Jupiter. The moon's surface was a beautiful brown and blue with long, straight lines crisscrossing its face. The dark areas on its icy shell were huge patches of sulfur, thrown off Io and caught by Europa. This moon was the smoothest object in the solar system due to the ice. As the sulfur and ice reacted together, water would erupt through cracks from beneath the surface and freeze instantly. Spacers sometimes referred to Europa as the cue ball of the Jovian system. The nickname wasn't too far from the truth. It was rare to find a crater on the moon's surface as it was constantly being replenished with fresh ice. Deep within the Jovian system, tidal forces from Jupiter and the other Galilean moons—Io, Ganymede and Callisto—were constantly tugging on Europa and providing the necessary internal heat to maintain its ocean. It was truly an alien environment.

Silhouetted against Jupiter, Hull could see a long, cylindrical object reaching out from the surface of the moon. The end of the object seemed to bulge out into two circular disks rotating opposite each other. This was Europa Prime: a massive space station attached to Europa by an immense tether. The tether contained dozens of space elevators that ferried visitors, personnel and equipment down to the main Europan settlement. It also served as the largest hose in the solar system as it brought water up from the surface to waiting ships. As they neared the station, Hull could make out several spacecraft already docked. Two were Victory class, while the other appeared to be one of the new Triumph class. A fourth ship was docked, but he didn't recognize the configuration. It wasn't standard UESA, whatever it was.

"Begin docking procedure," Hull commanded.

Cody nodded and placed both her hands lightly on the controls.

The Tereshkova began to ease into geosynchronous orbit with Europa Prime. The mighty ship used only its maneuvering thrusters to draw ever closer to the station. Above the dual spinning rings of Europa Prime were the docking ports. Looking like a crown on top of the station's head, the ports branched off into triangular arms that curved out into space. As the ship matched the station's orbit, it began to roll slightly to match with the docking ports. The station's docking arm began to extend toward the ship as well. As the two moved in perfect synchronization, a soft dock was achieved. Snapping off her thrusters, the Tereshkova was slowly brought into Europa Prime. As the docking arm snapped back into place, several of the stations' robotic arms extended and began attaching refueling hoses to the Tereshkova. A loud hiss echoed through the hull of the Tereshkova as the dock was pressurized.

Hull pushed his console forward and snapped off the harness. "Good flying, Lieutenant."

Cody smiled as she floated free of her console.

Hull twisted in the air and pushed off the back of his chair toward the main door. Hitting the release with his fist, he waited for the door to hiss open. Grabbing onto both sides of the frame, he looked back to make sure his crew were following suit.

Once satisfied, he returned his attention forward. "Let's go make sure our guest makes it off the ship." Tapping a button on his wristcomm, he lifted it to his mouth. "TC, meet us at the main airlock. Standard docking procedures."

CHAPTER THREE

"Are you ready to depart, sir?"

Vice President Wyman turned and laid his eyes on the hulking, metal form for the first time. Looking to be cobbled together from scraps of every shape and kind, it was nearly a foot taller than his six-foot form. Its red eye glowed ominously in the low light of the airlock. Two of his security men floated in front of the Vice President while five soldiers drew their weapons and took aim. "What the devil are you?"

"I'm sorry if I startled you," the massive mechanical form replied. Its voice seemed to be as mismatched as it was, sounding at times deep and resonating, while at others, barely above a squeak. Straightening up, it stepped into the light and dropped its arms to its sides. He stood on two squat magnetic legs that seemed insufficient to support his weight, but kept him tethered to the floor in zero gravity. Four giant pistons ran from the back of his calf piece to just below his hip. Each time he moved, stepped, or adjusted his weight, a small cloud of white gas was released from the valve. His triangular-shaped torso and cylindrical arms were grossly oversized compared to the rest of his body, while his oval-shaped head had only two features: a rectangular slit, which obviously represented his mouth, and a thin red eye that wrapped completely around his head. A singular bright spot on the slit indicated where he was looking. He was colored a rusty red and gold, while several of his parts had an almost metallic green paint job. Complete areas of the robot were uncovered, revealing the pneumatic pistons, shocks and wires that made it possible for it to move. "I am TC-10, the ship's counterpart."

The Vice President nodded and with a single gesture, let his men know it was okay to holster their weapons and stand down. Wyman took a step forward and patted the android on the chest plate. "Good to know you're on our side."

"Thank you, sir." The big bot whirred and rattled for a moment, looking as if it were about to fall apart. The smell of burning electronics began to fill the air. "I'm sorry," the bot stuttered as it's voice synthesizer malfunctioned, "I seem to be experiencing technical difficulties. Attempting to correct." TC-10 shook violently, but after a moment, shuddered to a stop. "Difficulty corrected. I am much better now, sir."

"That's good to know." Wyman took an initial step back, unsure about the pile of junk before him. It wasn't uncommon to see bots on these ships, but he had never seen anything like TC-10 before. It was made from a model preceding anything in his lifetime. The bots of today were slim, agile and very humanoid in appearance. Whatever mold had been used to create this monstrosity had hopefully, been broken and melted down.

TC-10 turned away from the Vice President's party and toward the airlock. Lifting its bulky, cylindrical arm, he retracted his three-pronged claw with a whirr of electrical motors. A panel snapped open on the top portion of its arm and a single silver tube extended. Inserting the tube into the control panel next to the airlock, TC's red eye rotated around and landed on the Vice President. "I'll have the airlock open in a few moments, sir."

A hissing sound behind the party caught the Vice President's attention. Spinning, he watched Captain Hull and his bridge crew maneuver into the airlock. "Captain Hull," Wyman said cordially, relieved to see TC's master arrive.

Hull floated into the small room and situated his body so he appeared to be standing vertically. "Mr. Vice President." He glanced over to see TC-10 working on the airlock. "I see you've met TC."

The Vice President nodded. "Where did you acquire this bot?"

Hull smiled. "TC and I have been together a long time. We've been through a lot of scrapes, but we've always made it through."

Wyman turned and looked at the big bot with awe. "Why didn't you upgrade your bot at the same time you did the ship's computer core?"

"Wasn't necessary," Hull said quickly. "I had programming installed in TC that allowed him to adapt and evolve. He just needed a little time to get 'acquainted' with the ship's new systems."

"You allowed your robot to evolve?" a soldier behind the Vice President asked. The disdain was clear in his tone of voice.

Wyman turned and saw who made the comment. Shooting him a quick cross look, he returned his attention to Hull. "Captain," he said slowly, never having intended to introduce the men standing with him, "this is Commander Trudeau. He and his unit have been assigned to accompany me by the Ministry of Defense."

"Commander." Hull placed two fingers on his brow and saluted Trudeau. Even though Trudeau was technically lower ranking than Hull, he was from a different branch of the government. MOD rank always superseded UESA. Even the lowliest ensign could take over an entire UESA ship in the event of an emergency.

"The airlock is ready for departure," TC-10 announced. Stepping back from the door, the big bot hunched down slightly and awaited instruction.

"Thanks, TC," Hull said as he moved toward the large circular hatch. Tapping the release button with his thumb, he watched the door roll open and a matching opening on the opposite side do the same.

Three members of station personnel dressed in the same blue UESA jumpsuits immediately met them. The lead man grabbed one hand onto the airlock hatch and extended his hand to the Vice President. He was balding with a thick, black mustache and goatee. His skin showed his slight Latin heritage. "Mr. Vice President," the man said with pride, "I am John Ramirez, Chief of Operations. Welcome to Europa Prime."

Wyman grabbed Ramirez's hand and shook it firmly. "Good to meet you, Chief."

"We're honored by your visit, Mr. Vice President," Ramirez continued.

"Since I've been the administrator here, only one other political figure has visited us."

"Oh?" the Vice President asked.

Hull could see Wyman's eyes glazing over slightly. He could tell the man hated this part of his job. As a lifelong soldier, he surmised Wyman would rather be standing knee deep in some trench filled with ice cold water rather than shaking hands and kissing babies. A quick grin flashed across the captain's face. He could respect Wyman for that.

"The President's Chief of Staff, George Rosenbaum," Chief Ramirez replied. "He was here about a year and a half ago."

"In that case," Wyman said with a smile, "I'm honored to be your second guest."

Chief Ramirez grinned broadly, obviously buying the load Wyman was peddling. "Let's get you and your team down to Europa Station."

"This isn't Europa Station?" one of Trudeau's soldiers queried the chief. "Oh, God no," the chief said with a smile. "What you're about to enter is Europa Prime. It's merely the docking port for the main station below. Europa Station actually sits on the ocean floor about fifty-five kilometers below the surface." Ramirez turned and motioned for the other men to follow. "I've already arranged for a tour of the facilities," he assured them.

Hull turned to Chris as the rest of his bridge crew floated past with the Vice President's team. "Chris, I need you and TC to see if you can figure out what the hell happened to number four engine."

The gruff engineer started to protest, but quickly stopped. He knew it would get him nowhere with Hull. "You got it, Skipper."

Hull patted Chris on the shoulder, then pushed off.

Chris grabbed onto the wall and turned to TC. "It's just you and me again, you old bucket of bolts."

TC's eye focused on Chris. "Look who's talking, you old fart."

Chris leaned his head back and laughed out loud. "I knew that whole polite crap was just for the benefit of the Vice President."

TC shook his metal head. "The captain said I had to be nice." Floating across the room, Chris patted the bot on the shoulder with another laugh. "Let's get down to engineering."

TC disengaged his magnetic feet and began to float freely in space. Arching his body forward, his legs snapped out and transformed into a second set of arms. Grabbing onto the surface behind him, he engaged his magnetic feet and hands and began to move like a spider along the wall. The two engineers disappeared through the hatch back into the Tereshkova.

***

Following the chief into the brightly lit station, Hull watched him float out through the circular docking shaft and hover above a large hole in the floor. Righting himself vertically, he pushed off the roof gently with his fingertips. Slicing through the air, they watched his body begin to slowly decelerate until he landed gently on the balls of his feet below. Walking across the floor, he tapped a silver intercom switch on the wall. "There are inertial dampeners between the ceiling and floor," his voice crackled through a nearby speaker. "It will take you gently from the zero g environment to normal gravity. All you have to do is jump."

As each man dove over the edge, they were righted by some unseen safety protocol so they landed gently on their feet. Once all were safely in the gravity of Europa Prime, the chief led them down a series of corridors until they reached the main embarkation room. Even though Hull had been to the station dozens of times, it never failed to take his breath away.

The entire room was immense. Completely circular with no sharp edges or corners, the bottom was entirely constructed of transparasteel, allowing an unparalleled view of Jupiter and Europa below. Dozens of circular tubes, also made of transparasteel, were grouped in the center of the floor. Glancing down through it, Hull could see that the tubes ran all the way down to the moon's surface and disappeared beneath the ice. Dozens of technicians worked at consoles situated around the room ensuring the safety of the travelers and the lifts. Hull watched three men and a woman climb into the nearest lift. As the door slid shut, the elevator began to sink away from Europa Prime. In less than ten minutes, the lift was rocketing back toward the surface. Hull watched it until it moved beyond his range of vision.

Turning to Kira, Hull smiled broadly. "I love this part."

"You're such a big kid," Kira laughed, "Captain."

Chief Ramirez started toward the lifts with the Vice President in tow. "What you see before you is what we like to call the 'Europa Express'," he said, laughing at his own joke. "This was designed to be the fastest and most efficient way to get to the station below." He pointed through the floor. "We're roughly two kilometers (one and two-tenths miles) above the surface right now. The entire trip takes roughly fifteen minutes from start to finish and is completely safe." Ramirez turned away from the Vice President for the first time since the airlock door opened. "Captain Hull, you and your bridge crew will have to take a separate lift. Is that all right?"

Hull nodded quickly, "We've all been here before. Give them the full tour." Ramirez smiled. Placing his hand on Wyman's back, he led him toward the first lift.

Hull turned and looked at his bridge crew. Jansen seemed to be sizing up the lifts nervously. "This is your first visit to Europa Station, isn't it, Ensign?"

Jansen nodded.

Hull laughed under his breath. "You're gonna enjoy this. Trust me." He looked over the lifts and pointed to two empty ones on the far side. "Katrina, why don't you and the ensign ride down together?"

Katrina smiled devilishly and nodded, completely understanding. "Yes, sir." Placing her hands on Jansen's back, she began to lead him toward the lift.

Hull and Kira watched the two youngest members of the bridge crew enter the lift. Jansen immediately grabbed onto the waist-high handrails with both hands and pressed himself against the curved wall of the elevator while Cody sat down Indian style in the center of the transparent floor. As the elevator was released from the top, it quickly began to accelerate. They listened to Jansen's scream until it disappeared into space.

Amidst the snickers of the deck crew, Kira slapped Hull across the shoulder. "You're such a jerk sometimes."

Hull laughed out loud as he headed for the second lift. "You've got to take some joy in your work," he said as they stepped into the lift.

Turning toward the wall, he placed his hands gently on the rails and stared off at the giant red planet hovering just beyond Europa. As it swirled endlessly amidst the storms that ravaged its unseen surface, Hull couldn't help but find the image beautiful. The orange, red and yellow bands of clouds rolled horizontally across the planet's face at different speeds, and every so often, he could see a bright blue flash of lightning reflected against them. He knew the surface had to be a hellish mixture of heat and pressure, but he didn't let that distract from the beauty it showed the galaxy.

As the lift was let go of its moorings at the top of the tube, he felt a moment of free fall before it was caught by the powerful magnetic field that suspended and powered it. Inertial dampeners built into the lift negated any negative gravity the ride was producing. As the lift picked up speed, he watched the silver bands that tied the tubes together whip by. Amidst the blackness that was space, he could see very few stars. The magnitude of Jupiter was all consuming. Tumbling around the gas giant, he could see asteroids that had been grabbed out of space and forced into orbit. Trails of dust ran across the sky forming Jupiter's planetary rings. They were minuscule compared to the next biggest gas giant in the solar system, Saturn, but they existed in a pristine condition only attainable in space. The dust, small rocks and ice that formed the rings tumbled and glittered in the reflected light of the planet. Looking below, he watched the ice ball that was Europa rushing up toward his feet. He could see the cracks crossing the surface and the areas of discoloration caused by the volcanic eruptions on Io. As he neared the moon, he could also make out a feature exclusive to this place: ice domes. Appearing to Hull like pimples on a teenager's face, the domes appeared in groups sporadically across the surface. They were caused when ice pockets of thermal water mixed with sodium bubbled up through the ice and was frozen instantly. They were almost all perfectly smooth and convex in shape.

The lift whizzed through the icy surface of Europa and plunged into darkness. What little light illuminated the Jovian system was quickly diminishing as the elevator descended beneath the five kilometers of ice. The blackness of the water and ice was all consuming. Hull had only experienced this kind of blackness while on Europa. It didn't exist anywhere else he had ever been. Even in the darkest areas of space, there was still the slightest hint of starlight to brighten the sky. Here, however, there was no reprieve. The darkness assaulted his senses.

Glancing down through the transparent floor, he could see a small bright dot in the darkness, glimmering like a pearl hidden away from man's view.

Amidst the sea of choking blackness, it was an oasis of respite, waiting with open arms to take him away from the cold. As the lift drew closer to the base, Hull began to make out the details of the massive manmade structure. It reminded him of pictures of viruses he had seen in its design. The main structure of the station was a white pancake-shaped building raised off the ocean's floor. Shooting off in all directions were smaller pancakes connected to the larger structure and each other via a network of tubes. Europa Station reflected the UESA's current "modular" design philosophy. It allowed for additional structures to be easily added if expansion was required. Europa Station also reflected one of the biggest construction projects ever undertaken by mankind. Bigger than Neptune and Earth Stations combined, it had nearly reached the vastness of the Moon Colony, although the moon had about a one-hundred-year head start.

Commissioned in 2312 as a joint venture between the governments of Earth, Mars and the United Earth Space Administration, Europa Station currently measured seventy-eight kilometers in diameter and was growing yearly. Not merely a research institute, although that was its primary mission, the station was also a main destination for tourists and a welcome layover for spacers hauling between Earth and Neptune Station. It had also become the key location in the solar system for xenobiologists. Not content with studying the bacteria found on Mars, the xenobiologists were determined to prove that life existed on the moon. Thermal vents in the ocean's floor mimicked conditions found on Earth, so the theory didn't seem that far-fetched. Built on stilts that were embedded deep into the rocky core of the moon, the bottom of the station was littered with lights that tried to penetrate the darkness.

Hull felt the lift begin to slow as it neared the exterior of the station. Through the brightly lit windows, he could see figures moving about. As the lift sank into the station, the transparasteel was quickly replaced by a solid white surface decorated with the logos of the UESA, Earth and Mars government. Slowing to a near crawl, the elevator set down into its base with a slight thump. As the lift was rotated to match the doors on the shaft, Hull and Kira stood straight and walked toward the exit.

The doors slid open in front of them revealing a brightly lit, bustling spaceport. People of all shapes and colors moved about the huge promenade deck for both leisure and professional reasons. Four stories high, the center of the room was filled with plants, bushes, and full-sized oak trees that reached high toward the circular stained-glass ceiling. Subtle lighting behind the glass sent soft rays of multicolored light filtering down on the plants and floor below. Built into the walls of each level were shops and restaurants of every kind. The promenade was designed to offer every amenity possible to travelers and permanent residents alike and to help visitors forget they were thirty miles beneath both water and ice on an alien world.

On the far side of the room, Hull spotted the entrance to Europa Station's biggest and most lavish hotel, the Dionysus. Kira had somehow wrangled rooms there for the bridge crew instead of their usual haunt, the Jupiter II (named not only for the ship in Arthur C. Clarke's 2001: A Space Odyssey but for the name of Europa used by Galileo when he originally discovered the moon). Hull hadn't asked how the feat had been accomplished, preferring not to look a gift horse in the mouth.

Rubbing the hair on his face, Hull looked for a long time at the front doors of the Dionysus. "I think I'm going to hit the shower. I need a shave."

Kira turned and looked at her captain without expression. "Yes, you do." She turned and spotted Cody and Jansen sitting on a small, white bench near the center atrium. She was rubbing his back as he leaned over with his head in his hands. "Our science officer doesn't look so good."

Hull nodded. "The first trip down the express is always the toughest."

Kira turned and looked at Hull just as a smirk quickly vanished from his face. Shaking her head, she started across the highly polished floor toward her crewmates. Squatting down in front of Jansen, she placed her hand on his knee. "How are you feeling, Ensign?"

Jansen groaned.

Hull moved past his crew and headed straight for the Dionysus. He had been in space for three straight weeks with nothing but MREs and recycled water. He was ready for a steaming shower, hot shave and a comfortable bed to sprawl out on. Making his way across the immense promenade deck, he stepped through the vaulted double doors into the Dionysus' lobby. Looking as if it were pulled straight out of the twenty-first century, it was decorated in faux white marble floors and deep, rich wooden walls. A grand staircase was in the middle of the lobby leading up to the second-floor restaurant and lounge. Three women stood to the right dressed immaculately in black formal wear. Two of the women were busily working on datapads as they took reservations.

The third woman, a beautiful blonde wearing a slinky black dress, walked up to Hull with her datapad cradled in her arm. "Welcome to the Dionysus. My name is Brigit. How can I be of service?"

A thousand crude thoughts erupted into the captain's mind at the request. Running his hand quickly down his face, he tried to focus. "I'm

Captain Alex Hull from the UESA Tereshkova. I believe I have several reservations."

Brigit smiled. "I'll check right now, Captain." She ran her hands skillfully over the datapad's touch screen. "I don't see anything," she said after a moment.

"It could be under my first officer's name," Hull suggested. "Look for Commander India Kira."

Brigit checked again and nodded approvingly. "I have it here. Is Commander Kira with you right now?"

Hull motioned over his shoulder with his thumb. "She'll be in shortly. I can sign for the rooms."

Brigit nodded once and quickly began altering the data on her pad. "Okay, Captain," she said, flipping the pad around to him, "I have you here for two rooms. If you can just place your thumb—"

"Wait," Hull interrupted. "Two rooms?"

"That's what I have here, Captain," Brigit confirmed.

Hull let out a long sigh. "That can't be right," he muttered mostly to himself. "Can you check the reservation again?"

Brigit nodded, her smile lessening a bit. "Of course, Captain." Keying in the information again, she stared at the pad for a moment before returning her attention to Hull. "The information is correct. The reservation was set three weeks ago by Commander Kira. Is there a problem?"

"Yes," Hull pinched the flesh just above the bridge of his nose, "we have five crew members and two rooms."

"Each room has two queen-sized beds," Brigit assured. "We can also bring a cot up from storage if you need it."

Hull closed his eyes for a moment. He would be sleeping on the cot tonight, guaranteed. "That will be fine," he said grudgingly after a moment. Reaching out, he pressed his thumb to Brigit's pad inside a small, blue rectangle on the screen. A quick red box appeared on the screen indicating it was authorizing his subdermal implant. The red box changed quickly to green with the words "Thank you" displayed prominently. Tearing the small paper receipt from the bottom of the pad, Hull stuffed it in his jacket pocket and turned away from Brigit.

"Do you need help with your luggage, Captain?" Brigit inquired.

Hull shook his head as he headed for the doors. "No, I have to go kill my first officer first."

***

Julie sat alone in a small, sterile room. A loose-fitting white t-shirt and a pair of baggy, drawstring pants had replaced her blue jumpsuit. This wasn't the first time she had been confined in a contamination situation, but each occurrence she hoped would be the last. It had been nearly three weeks since the incident and she had demonstrated no symptoms the research team had, yet they, or she assumed Jim, were unwilling to release her back into the station's population. Pulling her knees up to her chest, she crossed her arms over her knees and rested her head. Taking a long, deep breath, she slowly exhaled and tried to relax the tense muscles in her neck and back.

She heard the dual doors of the airlock hiss open. Lifting her head, she saw two men in complete environmental suits walking into her room. The blue light shining down through the helmet to illuminate the men's faces offset the deep bronze color of the suit. Not as bulky or restricting as the previous model, the new suits were slim, formfitting and allowed the greatest range of motion of any type used by UESA or MOD. Julie instantly recognized the second man in the door. "How are things, Quentin?"

Dr. Quentin Kelly was a tall and slender man, and the suit reflected that. She could make out the graying hairs on his goatee and barely see a few licking at his temples as well. His blue eyes looked unnatural under the light of the helmet, looking almost ghostly gray. "My team is leading the station's squash tournament."

"That's good news," Julie said conversationally. "Glad to hear it." Quentin and his assistant moved into the room as the airlock snapped shut behind them. Sitting down in the only chair in the room, he placed his hands on his knees and stared at Julie.

Julie felt as if his eyes were burning into her. "What? Are you expecting me to go into fits at any moment?"

Quentin shrugged. "Actually, yes. How do you feel?"

"The same as I did yesterday," Julie said evenly, "and the same as the day before that, and the same as three weeks ago."

"Getting a little cranky, are we?"

Julie looked at her colleague incredulously, "Wouldn't you? I've been stuck in this little room for three weeks and I've had to pee in more cups than I care to think about."

"Settle down," Quentin urged, patting the air with his gloved hands. "We're here to help."

Julie sighed and nodded slowly, "I've just been cooped up in this little room for too long."

"I know," the doctor said sympathetically, "but I have good news." Julie waited patiently.

"The Vice President is arriving today with a team of specialists," Quentin said with a slight bounce in his voice, "I have a good feeling you and Dr. Marcus will be out of quarantine by tonight, or tomorrow at the earliest."

Julie felt her spirits lift.

"All your tests have come back negative," Quentin continued. "You and Dr. Marcus have exhibited no similar symptoms as the research team did."

"Are they recovering?"

Quentin's face drooped, betraying his emotions. Julie's eyes went wide. "What the hell, Quentin?"

He looked to his assistant, then back at Julie. He bit his lip as he stared at his colleague. "No one told you?"

Julie felt the hairs on the back of her neck stand up. "Told me what?"

"I'm so sorry," Quentin said slowly, "three of the four men died about three weeks ago."

Julie gasped. "How?"

"We're still unsure," Quentin admitted. "They seemed to be recovering after you and Dr. Marcus intervened."

"But," Julie drew out the vowel in the middle of the word.

"But," Quentin echoed, "later that afternoon, three of the men starting having some kind of seizure again." He paused and took a breath, "Their hearts simply stopped. Resuscitation wasn't possible."

Julie fell back against the wall and stared at the ceiling. Swallowing hard, she tried to work some moisture into her dry mouth. This wasn't the news she wanted to hear.

"We did everything we could," Quentin said with a hint of guilt in his voice.

"I know."

"Those men were colleagues of mine," Quentin said quickly, "I wouldn't just let them die." He sounded more like he was trying to convince himself than Julie.

"I know, Quentin," Julie said strongly. "Wait," she paused, "there were four researchers."

Quentin nodded. "One is alive, but in critical condition. He can be very lucid one moment, but go completely off the deep end the next. It's really strange."

"Which one is alive?"

"Dr. David Jacobsen," Quentin breathed. "He was the lead archaeologist on the team and the man you and Dr. Marcus worked on."

A vivid flash of Dr. Jacobsen tearing at his eyes flashed into Julie's mind. Closing her eyes tight, she tried to push the image back into the deep recess from which it appeared. "When he's lucid, what does he talk about?"

“It’s odd,” Quentin said quietly, “he keeps on about some kind of alien civilization as far as we can tell.”

“What?”

“He keeps saying something about aliens,” Quentin reiterated. “He says he found—”

A knock on the large window in the front of the room interrupted him. Both he and Julie looked up to see a uniformed man beckoning for Quentin. Looking to Julie, Quentin shrugged in confusion. Standing up, he quickly moved through the airlock and met the uniformed man outside.

“Can I help you?” Quentin asked, staring at the man’s black uniform. He recognized it as Ministry of Defense, but couldn’t tell which rank.

“Dr. Kelly,” the man said slowly, “I’m from Admiral Wyman’s office.” His statement was very telling. Not referring to the Vice President by his current position spoke volumes about his allegiance. His build was standard military issue from the square jaw, to the tightly cropped hair on his head. He pulled a datapad from under his arm and handed it to Quentin. “This subject has just become classified.”

“I’m sorry,” Quentin said, accepting the pad, “and you are?” Glancing down, he quickly started to scan through the document in his hand.

“Commander Trudeau,” he said, retrieving the pad from Quentin. “Anyone caught talking about this subject without the proper clearance will be subject to the strictest laws of the MOD.”

“Dr. Sumner has the highest level of MOD clearance,” Quentin urged. “I’m sorry,” Trudeau said unemotionally, “neither Dr. Sumner nor yourself have the correct clearance.”

"What? I'm a P1," Quentin shouted. "That is the highest level of clearance."

Trudeau shook his head. "I'm sorry, doctor."

Quentin took a step back from Trudeau. Turning, he knocked on the window and motioned for his assistant to join him. "I'm taking this directly to Chief Ramirez. We'll see what he has to say about this lockdown."

"I assure you, doctor," Trudeau said with a smirk on his face, "Europa Station Chief Ramirez is completely aware of the situation and has assured the MOD of his complete cooperation."

Quentin swore under his breath. Motioning to his assistant, he charged out of the room without another word.

Trudeau turned and stared in the window at Julie. Pressing his finger to the small, black mic in his ear, he whispered something inaudible. Four men in black environmental suits burst into the room carrying several small, round devices in each hand. Trudeau motioned toward Julie and stepped back. The four men, their faces obscured by dark tinted visors, quickly headed into the first airlock. Waiting for the system to repressurize the lock, the men powered up the devices in their hands. With a hiss, the final door slid open.

Julie instantly recognized the devices in the men's hands. Standing up, she quickly threw herself against the wall away from the soldiers. "Who the hell are you and what are you doing?"

A raspy breathing noise from the men's regulators was her only response. She noticed the clearly marked MOD logo on each man's shoulder. She tried vainly to struggle free of the men's grip, but it was useless. There were too many of them.

Grabbing her by the shoulders, they pressed her against the wall of her cell. The first man pressed two of the small circular devices to each side of Julie's chest. Grabbing two more from the man behind him, he pressed them quickly to her thighs. Tapping the red activation button on the top of each, Julie felt electricity surge over her body. A high-pitched whine, much like a camera's flash recharging, filled her ears. Gritting her teeth, she felt her body become stiff as paralysis quickly set in. The devices were synapse inhibiters, known as "Syhibs". The syhibs sent out a strong electromagnetic field that disrupted the transmission of information between nerves. Certain spider and reptile venom functioned in a similar way. The syhibs also functioned as a personal shield, keeping any contagion she might have safely contained.

Dropping down to the floor, Julie found all she could move were her eyes. Glancing to the left, she saw the black clad men activating special devices on the chest plates of their suits that allowed them to touch her and not become paralyzed as well. The four men squatted down and grabbed Julie by the shoulders and feet. Lifting her like a board, they moved toward the airlock. Once outside, they stopped in front of Trudeau and awaited their instructions.

Trudeau looked at Julie for a long moment, then up at his soldiers. "Place her with the others, Lieutenant."

"Yes, sir."

The four men turned and quickly shuffled toward the lift at the rear of the room.

Trudeau watched until the men were in the elevator. As the doors slid shut, he reached up and keyed the mic in his ear. “We have the third subject,” he said evenly. He nodded once as he listened to the instructions in his ear. “Understood. We’ll have all three in moments.” Tapping the mic again, he listened to it chime softly twice to indicate it had gone into standby mode. Turning away from the containment room, he glanced over at the darkened windows of the lab.

As he tapped the lift’s call button, he shook his head. “I hate this friggin’ moon.”

CHAPTER FOUR

"Hey, TC," Chris yelled across the engineering bay, "come take a look at this."

"Just a minute, you old bat," TC-10 said as he placed a large pipe on the table in front of him. TC turned, dropped down and began to scuttle toward Chris' position. The engineering bay of the Tereshkova was the biggest area of the ship aft of the storage compartments. Cylindrical with a flat floor, it was located just about one hundred meters in front of the engines. From this bay, repairs or diagnostics could be performed on any of the engines or fuel lines that fed the cold fusion reactor. Huge pipes flanked both sides of the bay that delivered both water and deuterium to the engines. These were the veins of the ship. If one or more became blocked, the ship would basically choke to death. Giant support beams crisscrossed the engineering bay looking more like ribs and ligaments than manmade structures.

Stopping in front of Chris, TC lowered his head to the human engineer's level. "What am I looking at?"

"A fuel monitor," Chris said, handing the component to the bot. "What do you think?"

The bot took the fuel monitor, which was slightly smaller than a human hand, into his claw with the delicacy of a jeweler. Flipping the rectangular device, he focused on it with his glowing red eye. "That's interesting," he commented, "it seems to have been fused."

"What could cause that?" Chris asked, deliberately questioning the bot. "Very little," TC replied, shifting his attention to Chris. “These components are designed to withstand the most extreme temperatures and hostile environments. Plus,” TC paused and stared at the fuel monitor again, “the kind of heat needed to do this wasn’t present.”

Chris nodded, wiping his hands with a hand towel from his back pocket. “Theory?”

TC straightened up and seemed to be staring off into the distance. “Flashback.”

Chris patted the bot on his smooth, metal head. “The engine was beginning to flashback into the fuel line, the monitor detected it and shut down the line.”

“But in the process, it was fried,” TC finished the thought. “That’s why we lost power in number four as we were beginning docking procedures.”

Chris nodded. “It’s a damned good thing, too, or there’d be little bits of us orbiting Jupiter right now.”

“Actually,” TC said, placing the fused fuel monitor back on the small bench in front of Chris, “we would have been reduced to mere atoms by the resulting nuclear explosion. There wouldn’t be enough of us left to orbit anything, and we probably would have taken out most of the other ships in the area, plus a significant portion of Europa Prime.”

“You can sure suck the life out of a party sometimes,” Chris scolded. “I was just making a joke.”

“Not a particularly funny one,” the big bot argued.

Chris’ wristcomm chimed. “Tereshkova, you guys copy?” Chris motioned for TC to take the call.

TC pressed his claws to the side of his face, mimicking a behavior he had observed the human crew make often. "Captain Hull," TC greeted, instantly recognizing the voice.

"Hey, TC. Are you with Chris?"

"Unfortunately," TC said. "That was a joke, get it?" Chris groaned.

"Yeah," Hull said slowly. "Listen, we're staying at the Dionysus tonight. Our accommodations aren't the greatest, but at least we're not cramped up on the Tereshkova. That means you're on guard duty again, TC."

"Understood," TC replied.

"Did you guys figure out what happened to number four engine?"

"We tracked the problem to a fused fuel monitor," TC reported. "Flashback is the probable cause."

"Good work, guys. Hull out."

"Thanks, Captain," TC said proudly.

Chris tucked the rag back into his pocket. "Let's get that section of pipe replaced and get the hell out of here."

TC nodded. Standing straight, he moved back to his work area and grabbed the section of pipe off the table. Holding it gently with his claws, he walked quickly across the bay to where the old pipe had been removed. Sliding it into place, TC held the replacement piece in line with the rest. "Ready."

Grabbing the welder off TC's bench, Chris slid around the big bot and ignited the tool. A small blue light glowed to life on the tip of the pen-sized tool. Touching it to the seam between the pipes, instant weld began to form. Following the seam all the way around, Chris walked around TC and completed the weld on the opposite side. Snapping off the welder, Chris tossed it back on TC's bench and stood admiring his work.

"Your weld was ninety-eight point three percent effective," TC calculated as he scanned the pipe.

"Close enough," Chris grinned.

TC watched Chris turn and leave the engineering bay. Looking back down at the pipe, he retracted his claw and snapped open a small welding device on his arm similar to the one Chris had just been using. Igniting the tool, he ran it quickly around both welds, correcting the few minor flaws Chris had missed. Snapping his tool arm closed, he stood up and scanned his work. "One hundred percent effective," he said. Pleased with himself, he started toward the exit. Chris would no doubt be waiting for him.

"I saw that!"

TC spotted Chris standing in the doorway, his arms crossed. The big bot stopped dead in his tracks.

"You redid my work," Chris said, incensed.

TC sighed. "If you had done it right in the first place—"

"Don't give me that friggin' garbage, you overgrown Radio Shack project," Chris fumed.

TC shook his head and started back toward his crewmate. "It has come to my attention you are senile. I will have to report this to the captain."

Chris stared at the bot in front of him for a long moment. The anger that washed over his face suddenly broke and he laughed out loud. "Now that was a good joke."

TC patted his friend on the back. "You think I'm joking?"

"That's it. Go throw yourself into space."

"What's that?" TC said, moving out of the doorway, "My audio receptors seem to be malfunctioning. I didn't hear you."

Chris laughed. "That's because you're a bucket of bolts."

As the door slid shut to the engineering bay, the two could still be heard arguing outside.

***

Dr. Quentin Kelly sat alone in the waiting room. Sunk down in the curved, plastic chair, his arms were folded tightly across his chest. He had been waiting here for well over half an hour with no signs of change. Ramirez's administrative assistant, a young man with curly blonde hair, sat in the corner of the occupied office by a stack of datapads. As he finished one, he would set it aside and retrieve another from the pile. Quentin began to twist the hairs in his goatee between his finger and thumb. He stared at the door on the opposite side of the room, hoping that through some sheer act of mental will, it would open. So far, he hadn't had any luck. Letting out a long sigh, he let his head fall back against the wall. Two more minutes and he would leave, he assured himself. He didn't have to put up with this. He was the head of the biology department. "Yes, sir?"

Quentin turned to see the administrative assistant nod and listen to the small receiver in his ear.

"He's still here," the assistant confirmed. He nodded again and looked directly at Quentin. "Certainly, sir." Standing, the assistant moved across the room and stood in front of Ramirez's office door. "Chief Ramirez will see you now, Dr. Kelly."

Quentin stood and walked briskly to the door. "It's about damned time," he said gruffly to the assistant. "What's been holding him up?"

The assistant hit the door activation button. As it slid open, Quentin spotted the Vice President sitting in a chair opposite Ramirez's with armed security flanking him. He immediately understood.

Ramirez looked up and acknowledged Quentin. "Ah, just the man we wanted to see."

Quentin crossed slowly into the room and stood next to Ramirez's desk. "You wanted to see me, Chief? I thought I was here to see you."

Ramirez waved his hand, quickly dismissing Quentin's concerns. He pointed to the empty chair next to the Vice President. "Please, sit down, Doctor."

Quentin slid into the comfortable seat. He became aware of more than just the Vice President's security standing in the room. Glancing over his shoulder, he spotted Trudeau standing in the corner with two men garbed in black EV suits.

"Vice President Wyman," Ramirez said quickly, "this is Dr. Quentin Kelly, the head of Europa Station's biology research division."

Wyman extended his hand. "Good to meet you, Dr. Kelly." Quentin shook the Vice President's hand. "Likewise, sir."

"What does the biology station do here at the station?" the Vice President inquired.

"We're conducting a long-term study on the effects of prolonged space living. Even though our technology has advanced incredibly in the last century, we're still not sure if the human body can keep up," he said with the rehearsed tone of having given the same speech hundreds of times. "We're also working closely with the archaeology departments to identify any life, prehistoric or otherwise, here on Europa. That, along with various other projects, keep us fairly busy."

Wyman nodded. "Very good." The Vice President looked over his shoulder and exchanged glances with Trudeau. "Dr. Kelly," Wyman said slowly, adjusting his white dress uniform, "I have been told you've been working with the research team that encountered the artifact."

"Artifact?" Quentin looked curiously at Wyman and then to Ramirez. "I wasn't told anything about an artifact."

"I was assured he was up to speed," Wyman said to Ramirez with a hint of anger in his voice.

"I apologize, Mr. Vice President," the Chief said quickly. "I wasn't aware he hadn't been fully briefed. He has been working with the patients to determine if they were in anyway a threat to the station."

"That's right," Quentin said, trying to cover for his boss, "there hasn't been much time for meetings over the past month. My department had to find out if any of the four researchers or the two doctors and various nurses who were exposed to them after returning through decon were contaminated. If it was some kind of pathogen, we had to work quickly."

"You said the men had gone through decon?"

Quentin nodded at the Vice President. “That’s correct. They had each stepped out of the clean room into the main wet lab.”

The Vice President processed the information. “And they were clean?” Quentin nodded.

“Have any viruses, pathogens, or contaminants been found in any of the patients?”

“No,” Quentin said, shaking his head, “that’s what makes this whole thing so damned odd. Everyone’s clean, even the three members of the research team who died. When we performed a complete autopsy on each man, we found them to be in perfect physical health.”

Wyman rubbed his chin. “Any signs of drugs in their system?”

“All the screens came up clean,” Quentin answered.

“We have the toughest illegal drug screening program anywhere in the solar system,” Ramirez interjected. “All UESA and government employees are checked on a—”

One icy glance from Wyman stopped Ramirez midsentence. He wasn’t concerned with any of that. “In your professional opinion, doctor,” the Vice President wanted to choose his words very carefully, “why did these four researchers snap?”

Quentin took a deep breath and slowly exhaled. “That seems to be the million-dollar question right now, and nobody knows. I can tell you though that there was absolutely nothing wrong with any of the researchers, or the doctors and nurses exposed to them.”

Wyman smiled. “So you would clear a team who wanted to head out and investigate this artifact?”

Quentin shook his head. "I didn't say that. More research needs to be conducted. We should probably send a few probes or bots out first."

"Agreed," Ramirez said. "I can't authorize any more personnel being exposed to this…whatever it is. It's simply too great a risk."

"Let me tell you what the real risk is here, Mr. Ramirez: insurgents." Wyman let the statement sink into the thickening atmosphere of the room before continuing. "There are forces on Mars and Earth who live for no other reason than to topple our governments. These insurgents may have intercepted the message you so sloppily sent to Earth three weeks ago. They could be here right now."

Ramirez shook his head. "Why would revolutionaries care if we found some kind of artifact here on Europa?"

"These revolutionaries, as you call them, Mr. Ramirez, cling to different ideals than the rest of humanity." He looked at the station chief, then to Quentin, "You heard about the attack on San Angeles a week ago?"

Ramirez nodded.

"They killed nearly two hundred and fifty men, women and children because they claim we have encroached too far into the solar system," Wyman said grimly. "They feel we have no right to explore and colonize, that we are nothing more than conquerors intent on planting our flag on every piece of soil we can land on." He looked the two men squarely in the eyes. "If these insurgents were to find out some kind of civilization existed on Europa at some point in its history, they would finally have the proof they needed to begin swaying more, shall we say, 'like-minded' individuals to their cause."

"I see your point," Quentin breathed to Ramirez's dismay. "It's been so long since I've been on Earth, I had forgotten what it was like. I remember when they sabotaged the first launch of a Triumph class vessel."

Wyman nodded. "The rocket exploded on the pad, destroying billions of dollars in Earth technology and set back the Triumph program more than ten years."

"Not to mention thirty-four good men and women died that day," Quentin added.

Wyman sat forward in his chair. "We have to act now, Chief. If you don't authorize this mission, I will be forced to get presidential clearance and go over your head. One way or another, this mission will happen."

Ramirez glanced nervously from Wyman to Quentin. He had expected Quentin to be on his side, to help drive his point home. "Are you talking about covering this discovery up?"

The Vice President looked at the Station Chief for a long time. He didn't like the terminology he had used, but he was essentially correct. "We don't plan to hide this indefinitely, we just want to be sure of what it is before we make a decision. The clock is ticking, Mr. Ramirez."

"I can't be a party to a cover up," Ramirez answered quickly. "I won't." The Vice President grunted his disapproval. "It's already out of your hands. A presidential order will be here in a few hours and this mission will go ahead."

***

Hull leaned over on the chrome and aluminum bar and ran his finger around the rim of his glass. Looking around the supposedly “futuristic” dive, he stared at himself in the giant mirror that dominated the center of it—still no shower or hot shave. Lifting the squat glass, he took a gulp of the synthetic amber liquid. Cringing, he forced himself to swallow. Setting the glass aside, he ordered a soft drink to try and rinse the taste of the faux liquor out of his mouth.

“Still stuck at the Jupiter II, I see.”

Hull spun slowly in his seat to see a tall, brunette woman standing behind him. He glanced up and down her twice, then turned back to the bar. “Jennifer,” he greeted coolly.

Jennifer slid into the barstool next to Hull and signaled the bartender. The thin, golden bot behind the bar rolled up to the woman and placed two of his four hands on the bar. With his two extra appendages, he tossed a clean white towel over his shoulder. His slender head was designed with dual blue optical receptors, and a curved piece of metal that was supposed to resemble a mustache. “What can I get for you, pretty lady?” the bar bot asked pleasantly.

“I’ll have whatever he’s having,” she said, pointing to Hull.

The bar bot nodded and rolled back to the numerous colored bottles on the shelf behind the bar. Grabbing a clean glass with one hand, he lifted a clear bottle with the amber liquid off the shelf. Tossing it up in the air, he caught it with his other hand and held it upside down over the glass. Depositing the bottle back into its spot, he rolled up to the woman and placed it in front of her. Extending his open palm to her, she spotted the small, rectangular touch pad in the center.

With a nod, she pressed her thumb to the pad and paid for her drink. "Have a great day, pretty lady," the bar bot offered.

Jennifer took a sip of the drink and immediately set the glass back on the bar in disgust. "What the hell are we drinking?"

"It's supposed to be whiskey," Hull answered, "but it doesn't taste like it. Still messes you up just the same though."

"Any particular reason you're sitting in the Jupiter II's bar trying to get drunk?"

"Not trying. Succeeding." Hull shrugged as he played with his glass, "Seemed like the thing to do. Why is the captain of the newest Triumph class ship here?"

"Looking for you, actually," Jennifer admitted. "I heard you always stay here when on Europa."

"You just got lucky this time," Hull said, still not looking at the attractive woman to his left. "I'm actually staying at the Dionysus this trip."

"Very posh," Jennifer said, taking another drink of the synthetic whiskey. "How'd you wrangle that?"

Hull shrugged again. "Don't really know. Kira worked some kind of mojo. I'll pay for it somehow though," Hull admitted, fully understanding his particular breed of luck.

"You weren't the sunny kid in school, were you?" Hull grunted.

"You know," she said slowly, "I have yet to thank you."

"For what?" Hull asked, finally turning to face the woman.

"You turned down command of the Armstrong. I was the UESA's second choice for captain. If you hadn't," she took another sip of her drink, "I might be commanding the Tereshkova instead of you."

"But you're trapped in that brand new Triumph class ship." Hull swallowed the rest of his drink. "Life's rough for you."

He started to stand up, but Jennifer grabbed his arm. "Wait, Alex."

"Please take your hand off me, Captain," Hull said resolutely. "I have duties to attend to."

Jennifer grabbed Hull and physically forced him back in his seat. "I'm sorry, Alex," she said as sincerely as possible, "I didn't mean for it to come out that way. I was actually trying to thank you."

"Yeah," Hull spat, "I got that."

"Why do you have to be such an ass? Why can't you simply accept my gratitude?"

"Because I don't deserve it," Hull admitted. "All I did was turn down the posting. I didn't recommend you or anything. I just turned it down."

"I have to know," Jennifer said after a moment, "why did you pass on the Armstrong?"

Hull turned from Jennifer back to his empty glass. "I don't know."

"Come on," Jennifer urged, her hand still on his arm. "You have to know why."

Hull shrugged. "I was happy on the Tereshkova. I don't need to be on the nicest, fastest ship in the fleet to be content."

"Don't give me that line of crap," Jennifer said quickly. "I know you better than that. What really happened?"

Hull frowned. "That really is the honest-to-God reason. I'm happy where I am."

"That's why you're sitting in the Jupiter II getting drunk, right?"

"That's right."

Jennifer looked at Hull for a long time trying to see what was happening behind his eyes. "Okay," she breathed.

Hull nodded, saying nothing. He snapped his fingers signaling the bar bot. Once he had the bot's attention, he pointed to his empty glass.

Jennifer watched the golden bot slide over to Hull's position, refill his glass and take payment. She couldn't help but stare at the scruffy man in front of her. He looked broken, almost beaten down by the world. She felt deep pity for him. Here was a man who had excelled through the UESA, had been named one of the youngest captains in the history of the organization, and now was sitting in a twenty-year-old ship running parts back and forth to Neptune Station. Didn't seem fitting somehow. She wanted more for him. Grabbing his arm gently, she stood. "Let's get out of here."

"I just got a new drink," Hull argued.

Jennifer pushed the glass away. "Come on." Hull nodded grudgingly. "Where are we going?" Jennifer smiled. "For a walk."

Slipping her arm around his, she maneuvered him toward the exit. The bar bot quickly cleaned up the glasses and lifted two of his arms and waved. "Please come again, Captain Hull."

Jennifer Hull smiled over her shoulder. "Thank you."

Stepping out into the Jupiter II's lobby, she walked Hull toward the main doors. Once outside,

Hull lifted his hand to shield his eyes from the brightness of the promenade deck. Jennifer pushed Hull into a bench on the second level overlooking the atrium and sat down next to him. Rubbing his shoulder, she smiled softly.

"Are you ready to tell me what's really wrong?"

Hull glanced up with a defeated look on his face. "Today's my birthday." Jennifer stifled a small laugh. "Is that what this is all about? You getting older?"

Hull nodded, embarrassed. "How old are you?"

"Forty-two."

Jennifer's resolve broke and she laughed out loud. "Oh my God, alert the authorities," she said mockingly, "there's a forty-year-old man here!" She stopped and shook her head in disbelief. "That's it?"

Hull nodded, somewhat incensed at her tone. "See, this is why I divorced you."

"You divorced me?" Jennifer laughed again, "If I remember correctly, I think I began the proceedings."

Hull shrugged. "I'm old."

"You're only as old as you feel," Jennifer said, spouting the tired birthday adage before she even realized it.

"Then I feel older than dirt," Hull responded without missing a beat. "Why are you doing this for me? Aren't you supposed to hate me or something?"

"Just because I'm your ex-wife doesn't mean we have to be enemies," Jennifer pointed out. "We just weren't the best married couple. We were always good friends though," she smiled. "Our jobs just took us in different directions, that's all."

Hull nodded, remembering the exact circumstances that led to the divorce. He looked up into her soft eyes. "I miss you sometimes."

She rubbed his back. "I miss you sometimes too, but then I remember what a drama queen you are and I get over it."

Hull scowled. "Wench."

Jennifer smiled playfully. "Jackass."

"Come on," Jennifer said, standing up. Reaching out, she offered her hand to her ex-husband.

"Where are we going now?" Hull took her hand and stood up.

"I'm taking you out to dinner for your birthday, but first," she turned toward the Dionysus, "we're going to go get you cleaned up."

Hull laughed despite his mood. "Yes, Captain."

CHAPTER FIVE

The room was cool and dark. A few stray lights littered the ceiling while an odd blinking green light cast an evil glow across the floor. Three men gathered around a single monitor, its blue light silhouetting them. They stared at the image frozen on the screen for what seemed like an eternity. No one had the words to speak, or the verbiage to describe what they were seeing. One of the men pulled away from the screen, placed his hand on his forehead and began pacing behind the other two men. Finally, the silence was broken.

"When did you say this was intercepted?"

"Three weeks ago."

"And we're just seeing it now?"

"It got lost in the shuffle. Earth Gov sends a lot of transmissions."

"We have to act on this. It was marked for the President's office." Agreed, but what are we going to do?"

"We have to take it away from them. We have to show it to the rest of humanity."

"How?"

Another long silence descended over the room as the men returned their gazes to the frozen image of the artifact discovered on Europa. The green image filter used on the camera made it seem even more otherworldly. Staring at the black lettering, they let their eyes wander down to the humanoid face partially buried in the silt. A bit of disturbed mud, probably from the photographer's footsteps, was wafting up around the face making it look smoky. As it lay sideways in the mud, it seemed to be calling out for their help to rescue it from its watery grave.

The men finally stood and addressed one another. “We have to take it from them.”

“By force?”

“By force. Alert our contacts on Europa.”

***

Dr. Jim Marcus leaned on the edge of the table with his arms folded. Taking a long breath, he let his head fall forward onto his forearms. Three weeks ago, he had been a respected scientist with a bright future ahead of him. Now he was hidden away in a part of the station he had never seen before with three dead bodies, a man in an intensive care unit, three nurses and Dr. Sumner lying motionless on a cot on the far side of the room. This wasn’t exactly where he thought his career would end up.

Glancing up, he looked from one nurse to the next. The first was reading a discarded pad she had found, while the second was trying to sleep. The third nurse, a pretty young woman with messy brown hair, was sitting on the floor next to her bed with her knees tucked up against her chest. Jim recognized this nurse as the one who had helped him in the wet lab. He wanted to walk across the room and sit with her, tell her everything would be all right, but he couldn’t bring himself to lie. How could he be sure of that himself?

His eyes wandered from the nurses to the three men in black body bags. They were arranged parallel to each other on the floor just in front of the intensive care unit. Each rectangular bag was zipped up tightly and tagged with the men's names. Seeing them for the first time today, he had been in shock. The last time he had seen the men was on the floor of the wet lab, apparently stable. None of the body bags were hermetically sealed and there weren't any biohazard tags present so he could only assume that whatever they contracted while in the Europan ocean wasn't contagious. At least that assuaged some of his fears.

Standing up, he leaned back against the wall with his hands folded behind his back. The low, repetitive hiss of mechanically assisted breathing filled his ears. From time to time, he found he could ignore it. At other times, it was all he could hear. He turned and stared at the intensive care unit situated almost exactly in the center of the floor. Large with angled sides, the top was constructed of thick transparasteel allowing doctors to see in and check on the patient. Two long canisters situated on each side of the box fed oxygen into the chamber and scrubbed the carbon dioxide created by the patient. Jim could see tubes of all kinds running from the side panels into the body of the archaeologist. A constant cringe was pasted onto his face displaying to all that he was in pain. His eyes were bruised and scabbed where he had tried to scratch them out. He seemed to be in some kind of coma, either naturally or chemically induced—Jim couldn't be sure which. He wished the archaeologist would wake up, even for a moment, to tell them what had happened. Or to at least give them some clue of what was beneath all that water.

A low moan caught Jim's attention. Snapping his head around, he saw Julie move for the first time since she had been brought in by black-clad stormtroopers. Of course, he realized they were merely men in EV suits, but they had an air of danger and authority about them. Perhaps it was the pulse pistols strapped to their legs, or the darkened visors, but he hadn't even tried to get in their way as they exited and locked the door behind them. Charging across the room, Jim dropped down next to the cot. She slowly lifted her arm, but let it flop almost lifelessly over the side. Turning her head, she tried to focus on her colleague.

"Jim?" Her voice was gravelly.

"I'm here." Jim could tell it hurt Julie to speak. Lifting her hand, he held it in his and softly caressed her arm. "Just rest." He watched her pupils dilate as they tried to adjust to the lighting in the room. He understood. When she had been brought in, she had been restrained with syhibs. The side effects of the synapse inhibitors often lasted well beyond the removal of the devices.

"Why are they doing this?" Julie gasped, trying to regain control of her body.

Jim shook his head. "I don't know."

"We're not even contaminated," Julie said quietly.

Jim's eyes widened slightly, but he had already surmised the same. "How do you know?"

"Quentin told me," she replied. She writhed a bit as she tried to regain control of her faculties. "We and the research team are clean."

"Are you sure?"

Julie nodded as best she could.

Jim's eyes wandered over to the three body bags in the corner. "Then what killed those men?"

Julie tried to say something, but couldn't push the words from her mouth. Taking a slow breath,

Jim watched her eyes flutter and roll back into her head. Her hand became limp.

"Don't do this," he said nervously. Pressing his fingers to her throat, he searched for a pulse. Holding for thirty seconds, he counted a steady beat. Watching her chest rise and fall, he leaned his ear close to her mouth and listened to her breathe. She wasn't responding, but her vitals were strong. She had just slipped from consciousness again. Not surprising after having four syhibs attached to her. One would have done the job. Four were overkill and a bit sadistic.

The nurse who had been curled up next to her bed quickly moved to Julie and Jim's side. Standing over his shoulder, she looked down at Julie. "Is she okay?"

Jim glanced up at the nurse, unaware of her approach. "I really don't know. Her pulse is strong and she's breathing, but beyond that, I couldn't tell you."

The nurse nodded. Taking a step back, she leaned against the table that occupied this side of the rectangular room. "What's happening to us?" she asked quietly.

Jim ran his hand over Julie's forehead tenderly, "I wish I knew. Seems we were all in the wrong place at the wrong time."

"That isn't very comforting," the nurse replied.

"Sorry," Jim responded. "By the way, I'm Jim. Jim Marcus."

"Sue," the nurse replied.

"Just Sue?" Jim asked, "Nurse Sue?"

"Sorry," she replied, "Sue Kithara."

Jim nodded. He looked at the young nurse. "Julie told me that none of us are infected. The doctor who was helping us, Dr. Kelly I think his name is, told her that we were clean, even those men who died."

Tears welled up in her eyes. "Why are we being kept here then?"

"We're going to make it through this, Sue," Jim said, turning away from Julie, "but we're all going to have to stick together. Do you understand?" Sue wiped the tears from her eyes and nodded.

Jim reached over and placed his hand on her shoulder. "We're going to be okay. I promise." He was doing the one thing he didn't want to do.

***

Hull and Jennifer sat smiling at each other at a small table deep within the Dionysus' most luxurious restaurant, the Calydon (continuing the tradition of naming places and objects in the Jovial system after Greek mythology).

Designed with luxury and style, the Calydon had become one of the most expensive and sought-after reservations in the solar system. The interior was richly decorated and small lights on the tables and walls were dimmed and flickering to simulate candlelight. Soft music wafted through the restaurant that Hull had identified as early eighteenth century. The restaurant was nearly filled to capacity tonight with families and couples seated at every available table.

Hushed conversations could be heard mingling in the air, and the sharp clank of silverware against the plates created an almost musical sound.

It seemed fate was on Hull's side this night. He and Jennifer had intended to eat at one of the other restaurants on the promenade deck, but had stopped by the Calydon on a whim. The maître d' had just received a stern lecture from the hotel's owner in front of several patrons. In a huff, he had given away the reservation belonging to the owner's best friends, who were no less than two minutes late, to Hull and Jennifer. It was all a matter of being in the right place at the right time. The maître d' would surely be fired, but he didn't care, he had informed the two as he seated them. He was sick of working on this moon anyway. As he handed each their menus, he explained he would head home to Mars and start his own restaurant. Very insistent, he made Hull and Jennifer promise they would stop and dine there on their next trip to Mars.

"I can't believe we're eating dinner at the Calydon," Jennifer said, taking in the atmosphere.

"This is nice," Hull agreed.

She was dressed in a long, red, strapless and sleeveless gown she had purchased on her last trip to Neptune Station. She'd been dying for an occasion to wear it, and this was as good as any. She had pulled her hair up behind her head except for a curly strand that hung down the left side of her face. Hull couldn't believe how radiant she looked. Maybe it was time, or the distance, but a haze had developed over his memory in the five years since the divorce was finalized. He didn't remember how beautiful she was and he stared at her as she lifted her wine glass and took a sip.

Setting the glass down, Jennifer smiled at her ex-husband. She had done a pretty good job of dressing him. Having taken him to his room, she sat him down in the bathroom and completely shaved his face. She had even trimmed his hair slightly, just to knock off the rough edges. After all, she knew how he liked it. A quick call to the hotel's clothing shop and she had secured him a black suit cut in the latest style. Wearing a gray shirt beneath his jacket, Jennifer had picked a black silk tie from the shop to complete the package. He cleaned up very well.

The two sat in silence for a moment just looking at each other. The conversations and music around them seemed to die away, leaving them completely alone. In that instant, all memories of the fights, pain and divorce were wiped away, leaving only the teenagers who had first met on Earth during their academy days. Reaching across the white tablecloth, Hull placed his hand tenderly on hers. He smiled when she didn't automatically recoil.

"Happy birthday," Jennifer whispered. "Thank you," Hull answered.

"So is today turning out better than you thought it would?" Jennifer asked as she stared at his hand upon hers.

Hull nodded with a sly smile. "So far." He lifted his glass and took a drink of the finely aged merlot. Savoring the taste for a moment, he finally swallowed the true alcohol and immediately felt the warmth spread down his esophagus and into his stomach.

"So do you have a birthday wish?" Jennifer asked, trying to lead the conversation.

"Same one every year."

Jennifer laughed. "You can't be serious. Are you still asking for that?" Hull smiled deviously.

"Don't you think you should give up on that wish by now?"

"No," Hull said quickly. "How great would that be if I could choke people with a mere thought?"

"Like Darth Vader?"

Hull nodded. "That would be incredible. Don't like your assignment? Choke your boss. Don't like your hotel accommodations? Choke your first officer," he allowed himself a brief smile. "Wouldn't that be great?"

"I really think you need to stop watching those films. They're nearly what," she paused, trying to remember when the film was released, "three hundred years old?"

"Three hundred and forty-three," Hull corrected.

"They're not even considered classics anymore," Jennifer laughed, "they're antiques."

Hull waved off the conversation, "We're not getting into this again. I like Star Wars and you don't. Enough said."

"It's not that I don't like them," Jennifer corrected, "it's just that they're goofy. I can't take all that mystical Force mumbo-jumbo seriously."

"No imagination," Hull laughed.

"Come on," she argued, "samurai-like warriors that use laser swords in an age of starships and energy weapons? You have to see the ludicrousness of that."

"I'm not talking about it anymore," he huffed.

Jennifer laughed out loud. She couldn't remember the last time she had this much fun. The two fell into a comfortable silence again as their eyes locked.

"Why did we get divorced?" Hull asked finally, breaking the silence. Jennifer sighed. "Not this again. I don't want to go there tonight. I'm having a good time with you, Alex, please don't ruin it."

"I'm not trying to ruin anything," he defended himself. "I'm having a good time, too. That's why I asked. We were pretty good together."

"You're just trying to sweet talk me to get under my dress."

"That's lovely." Hull laughed. "You've been in space too long, sweetheart." Jennifer shook her head. "Why do you always have to bring this up when we're together? Why can't we just have a nice night?" Hull bit his lip. "Because I honestly miss you."

The smile faded from Jennifer's lips as the happiness drained from her face. "Don't you remember the fights we had? It seems like that's all we did. Plus," she pointed out, "we never were together. You were always on your ship, and I was on mine. That doesn't make for the healthiest relationship."

"We can do things differently this time. Either one of us could transfer. We're not too old to start again," Hull persuaded.

"You know damn well that isn't going to happen. Are you going to give up your command for me? I'm not giving up mine for you, Alex. The problem with us is that we both know exactly what we want, and we worked our butts off to achieve that. Unfortunately, some of those wants, namely us, had to be sacrificed." Jennifer took a long breath. "We can't change that now."

"I know, I know," Hull said quietly. "I just have to try." He took her hand into his and smiled. "I'm just a sentimental old bastard tonight."

Jennifer chuckled. "Sweet though." She quickly lifted her head and glanced around the restaurant. "We don't belong here."

Hull nodded with a smile.

Jennifer smiled seductively. "You want to skip dinner and head right into the birthday sex?"

Hull ripped the napkin from his lap and tossed it on the table. Standing up, he lifted Jennifer from the table. "I thought you'd never ask."

CHAPTER SIX

Trudeau paced the floor in front of the video screen. Behind him and seated on a comfortable couch was the Vice President. His white uniform jacket was unbuttoned down the center revealing the white dress shirt he wore beneath. Rubbing his nails on his pant leg, he tried to regain some of the sheen that had been there before the trip. Space travel was anything but clean, especially when you were required to travel on an over glorified garbage scow like the Tereshkova.

Leaning his head back into the thick cushions, he stared at Commander Trudeau and remembered his glory days in the Ministry. At one time, he had the same physique, the same chiseled chin and the same air of prim and proper military life. During his tenure behind a desk, he had lost that somewhere. He had stopped caring about military protocols in favor of impressing those in the government he worked with. It had been successful though. He was now the Vice President of the United Earth Government, but did that really mean anything to him? He would much rather be out charging front lines with a pulse rifle in his hand instead of shaking the hands of delegates and fathers of sixth grade students who had written history reports on him.

He was a figurehead. He knew that, although his ascension to the office had been quite a coup, he had only been a gesture made by the President for the citizens of Earth and Mars. The President's continued pledges to fight the insurgents and return peace to the planet had required a face. He had chosen Wyman: a highly decorated soldier with over forty years of service under his belt. The President fully expected the Vice President to be the new face of his war, but Wyman had other ideas. He would find a way to reinvigorate the military after the past few administrations had cut it in favor of funding exploration through the UESA. If this war had taught Wyman anything, it was that the enemy didn't always come from beyond our borders. Sometimes, the enemy was in our own backyard. He wanted this administration to be prepared for that, even if it meant taking up a rifle himself and standing the first watch.

"Would you stop pacing?" Wyman said finally. "The call takes a few minutes to connect."

Trudeau quickly realized what he had been doing. "Sorry, Admiral. I'm just a little anxious."

"Understandable," Wyman replied. Pointing to a seat in front of the sofa, he motioned for Trudeau to sit down. The commander quickly complied.

The quarters Chief Ramirez had assigned the Vice President were easily the largest and most luxurious of all the crew's. Wyman could have easily stayed at the Dionysus, but security in this portion of the station was much tighter. Few outside the President's office knew about this unscheduled visit to Europa. It was a high risk sending such a visible figure on this mission, but President Wilson would have it no other way. Wyman admired him for that. Wilson, like Wyman, was a very hands-on kind of leader. If he couldn't be there himself, his number two in command would be.

The Ambassador Suite, as these quarters had been nicknamed, was larger than even Ramirez's. Situated in pod three of the station, it rivaled the size of the main biology lab. Decorated with the latest styles and fashions from Earth and Mars, bold shades of deep red and black colored the room. A plush black fabric Wyman wasn't familiar with dominated the furniture. It was softer and yet tougher than cotton, with almost the consistency of suede. A light tan carpet, which usually wasn't allowed in the station, complimented the wall and furniture color almost perfectly. Large portions of the far wall were made of transparasteel to allow guests to gaze out into the Europan ocean. Huge banks of lights had been installed above the windows on the outside of the station to illuminate some of the terrain of the moon. Wyman couldn't understand why they had gone to the trouble. Light brown mud in every direction and the occasional scientist passing by was all that was visible. It really wasn't much to look at. Perhaps it was enough to see this alien terrain, but for Wyman, it was just a big ball of mud, water and ice. He suddenly wished he was back in San Angeles.

The video screen in front of him suddenly blinked to life. It displayed the seal of the President against a dark blue background before it faded and was replaced with an image of the Oval Office. The President's face slowly came into view.

Sitting up on the couch, Wyman quickly adjusted his jacket and tried his best to look official. This was, after all, his boss. "Mr. President," Wyman greeted.

"Jesus, Jack," Wilson said quickly. "You've only been on Europa for seven hours and it seems like you've pissed off half the population." He held up several reports. "Chief Ramirez wants to hang you from a goddamned yardarm."

“Sir,” Wyman started to apologize, “I can explain—”

The President waved him off. “There’s no need. I’m on your side, Jack.” Wyman felt instant relief.

“I want that artifact, whatever it may be, secured and on its way back to Earth by this time tomorrow,” the President stated.

“Sir, with all due respect,” Wyman clasped with hands together, “we don’t even know how big the artifact is. All we have is a photo with no point of reference. It could be six inches tall, or ten feet.”

The President shook his head. “My people tell me from what they have determined, it’s about six feet tall by using the information embedded in the photo, such as the zoom level and the position of the camera on a standard EV suit.” He leaned toward the camera. “The only thing we don’t know is if it’s alone.” Wyman nodded. “What if there are more? We could be looking at a serious operation here.”

“We’ll have to cross that bridge when we get to it,” the President responded. “Right now, your one and only task is to recover the artifact and ship it back to Earth aboard the Tereshkova.”

Wyman cursed under his breath. “Couldn’t we use a different ship?”

“Absolutely not,” Wilson said emphatically. “The crew of the Tereshkova have already gone through all the screening and psychological tests. We don’t want to waste time on another crew. They’ve already got the clearance for the mission.”

“Understood,” Wyman said with a nod.

“Get in there tomorrow morning and recover the artifact. I want the Tereshkova launched for Earth by tomorrow night. Are we clear?”

Wyman nodded again. The video screen blinked off as the President severed the connection. Leaning back in the sofa, he took a minute to process the orders. His gaze slowly wandered the room, but finally settled on Trudeau. "Get your team ready, Commander."

Trudeau stood up and snapped to attention. "Yes, sir. Will you be accompanying us on the mission, Admiral?"

Wyman rubbed his chin and took a breath. "I don't think so. I've spent enough time in EV suits in my lifetime. You and your men are more than capable of handling the mission, right?"

Trudeau nodded. "Yes, sir."

"I want to meet in the main wet lab tomorrow morning at oh six hundred." Wyman saluted the man half-heartedly. "Dismissed."

Trudeau returned the salute and headed toward the door. As the commander exited the room, Wyman pulled off his jacket and laid down on the couch. Propping his feet on the black pillows, he took a long breath and slowly exhaled. Tomorrow was going to be a very long day.

***

A knock on the door startled the two. Cody turned to Kira, then slowly slid out of bed. Glancing at the digital clock on the wall as she passed, she groaned. Turning on the room's lights, she adjusted the tight gray tank top she wore to cover her exposed midsection. Pushing her hair back, she tapped a button on the console next to the door. A small rectangular window of one-way transparasteel appeared in the center of the door.

Glancing through, she sighed and turned back to Kira. "It's Jansen."

"I don't want the green eggs," Kira mumbled from under her covers, obviously still in the middle of a dream.

Cody could only surmise Kira was deep in Dr. Seuss' world. Turning back to the door, she unlocked it and hit the release button. "Do you know what time it is?"

"No," Jansen replied, "should I?"

Jansen's uniform was unzipped to about the waist. He had pulled off the top portion and tied the sleeves around his midsection exposing the tight, white t- shirt he wore beneath.

Cody reached down and grabbed Jansen's left arm. Lifting it up, she turned his watch to face him. "It's nearly two thirty in the morning!"

"Don't shout," Jansen warned her, "there are people trying to sleep. It is two thirty in the morning, you know."

Cody looked at Jensen for a long moment. She didn't know whether to slap him and send him away or laugh out loud. Luckily for him, she chose the second. "What do you want, Ensign?"

"I'm bored sitting in my room," he said, leaning against her doorframe. "I want to go out and I was hoping for some company."

"You are aware of the captain's policy on crew relationships, right?" Jansen nodded, "I've heard the speech." He took a step back from her.

"That's not what I have in mind. I just want some company."

"…Not eat them on a goat," Kira mumbled as she rolled over. Jansen stared at his first officer curiously. "What's with her?"

Cody shrugged and smiled. "She doesn't like green eggs and ham."

"Who does?" Jansen laughed. "So you want to go with me?"

Cody looked at the young man standing outside her door. This wasn't like her at all. She was always in bed at exactly nine. That was probably why she decided to go. "Sure."

Jansen clapped his hands once in excitement. "Great!"

"Let me just get some pants on," Cody said as she closed the door. Rushing across the floor, she moved toward the small table near the rear that held her duffel bag. Quickly zipping open the top, she retrieved a pair of jeans and pulled them on. Slipping on her work boots, she tucked her jeans over the top of them. Glancing at her herself in the mirror, she frowned. Reaching up, she pulled the rubber band from her hair. Shaking her head, she reached up and ran her fingers through her hair. Opening her eyes again, she stared at her new hairdo. It was wild, she thought and smiled, and attractive. Grabbing a pad from her nightstand, she scrawled a quick note on it and left it next to Kira's pillows. Rushing to the door, she opened it again and stepped outside. Slipping her arm around Jansen's, she led them away from the room. This wasn't like her at all, and she liked it.

"So what did you have in mind, Ensign?"

Jansen pulled a flier out of his pocket and handed it to Cody. "It's called 'Club Io'. It's supposed to be the place to be on Europa."

"You're taking me to a nightclub?" Cody asked as she skimmed over the yellow flier.

Jansen stopped and looked down at his companion. "Is that okay?"

Cody folded the paper, stuck it in her pocket, turned and smiled broadly at Jansen. "You bet."

***

Hull rolled over and tried to catch his breath. He hated to admit it, but he wasn't in the best shape anymore. Glancing to his right, he stared at Jennifer's nude form on the floor next to him. Reaching over, he caressed her upper thigh. She quickly cuddled up next to him, wrapped her legs around his, and started to run her fingers through his chest hair. He smiled and looked around the room at the mess they had created. Tables and chairs were completely knocked over, while the bed had been completely stripped of its sheets. Pieces of clothing were strewn everywhere, including Jennifer's bra, which had somehow become entangled in the lights above the bed.

"How did we end up on the floor?" Hull asked with a laugh. "The bed was just too restricting." Jennifer smiled.

"I just can't get over this."

"What?"

"We're acting like first year cadets again."

Jennifer laughed out loud. "I seem to recall being a bit more flexible back then."

Hull felt a sore spot forming in his lower back and agreed. Running his hand down her arm, he laced his fingers with hers and held her hand. Letting his head fall back, he tried to enjoy the moment, but the nagging voice in the back of his mind appeared again. Trying his best to ignore it, he turned and stared at Jennifer. A light coating of sweat covered her body causing it to glisten in the lights.

Placing her hand tenderly on his cheek, she leaned in and kissed him. "Happy Birthday."

"Technically," Hull breathed, "it's not my birthday anymore."

"Close enough."

The voice in the back of Hull's mind had moved to the front and was screaming at him. He couldn't ignore it any longer. "Jennifer," he said slowly, "I'm going to give up my commission."

She propped herself up on her elbow and looked curiously at her ex-husband. "Why?"

"So I can be with you again."

Jennifer frowned. "Who says you're invited?"

"What?"

"That was your idea," Jennifer reminded him, "not mine." Hull felt his heart sink. "What are you trying to say?"

Jennifer remained silent as a shadow of guilt passed over her face. His heart hit the bottom of his stomach with a plop. "Tell me."

Jennifer leaned back over on his chest. "Let's not talk about it. I just want to enjoy the night."

"No way." Hull pulled away from her. Standing, he moved to the side of her hotel room and grabbed the two discarded chairs and righted them. Grabbing his boxers off the floor, he pulled them on and sat down in one of the chairs.

Pointing first to Jennifer, he then pointed to the second chair. "We need to talk. Right now."

Jennifer begrudgingly stood. Grabbing the bed sheet, she wrapped it around her body. Sitting down in the chair, she stared at Hull apologetically. "I didn't know you still felt this way."

"What way?"

Jennifer took a long breath. "I didn't know you were still in love with me."

Hull made no attempt to disprove her statement. "What's going on?"

"Alex," she let her head fall forward. "I'm getting married in a month."

The news hit Hull like a freight train. He quickly grabbed onto both arms of the chair to keep his world from spinning out of control. "Who is he?"

"A senator from Mars," Jennifer replied. "He's a good man," she defended herself, "and he's good to me."

"I knew today was too good," Hull said slowly, "There had to be a catch." He turned and looked at his ex-wife. "So you wanted one last fling before you got married again?"

"No, that's not it at all. I hadn't intended for any of this to happen. I just wanted to see you again," she said honestly, "just wanted to tell you the good news. You were always my best friend, Alex, and I guess I just needed your blessing. When I saw you this afternoon, I just couldn't help myself."

"How can you do this to me?"

"Get remarried?"

Hull nodded. "You were mine," he said almost pathetically.

"'Were' being the key word in that sentence. We're divorced, Alex," she stated blatantly. "You had to know that someday we would both move on."

"I know," Hull said through gritted teeth. "I know."

Jennifer reached over and placed her hand on his. "I do love you."

He turned and looked into her eyes. For a moment, he was lost, but his mind quickly returned to the situation. "I love you too," he replied.

"We'll always have Europa," Jennifer offered him. Hull patted her hand and nodded.

She turned and looked at the bed. "And we still have tonight."

Hull smiled, but shook his head. "I'm not really in the mood anymore."

"Why?"

"Earlier tonight," Hull started, "we were just two consenting adults. We had no attachments to worry about, but now I know you belong to another man. I just can't. It isn't right."

Jennifer sat back in her chair. She understood completely. "So what do you want to do now?"

Hull stood slowly and began to collect his clothes from the floor. Pulling on his pants, he turned and looked at his ex-wife. "I think I'm gonna go get a drink."

"Am I invited?" she asked, but already knew the answer.

Hull shook his head. "Not this time, sweetheart. I have a lot to think about and I could use some time alone."

"I understand."

Hull stepped in front of Jennifer and extended his hand. Lifting her out of the chair, he embraced her tightly. Running his hand down through her hair, he let it rest on the flesh of her back. "It was good seeing you," he said without letting go.

"Congratulations. I wish you all the happiness in the world."

Jennifer pulled away slightly with a single tear in her eye. Reaching up, she kissed Hull gently on the lips. "Thank you, Alex."

Finally letting go, he slipped on his shoes and threw his coat on. Turning away, he headed for the door. Tapping the console, he waited for it to slide open. As it hissed open, he paused. Placing his hand on the doorframe, the tiny voice in his mind urged him to turn around, to take one more look at her. He let his hand fall free of the door and stepped into the hallway leaving Jennifer standing wrapped in the bed sheet in the middle of the room. Alone.

CHAPTER SEVEN

Club Io was tucked in the far corner of the third level on the promenade. The white walls of the station gave way to Io's burnt orange color. A massive neon sign hung above the door with a live holographic image of Io rotating behind it. Two large windows were on either side of the door with a semi- transparent substance made to resemble lava flowing through each. As the lava flowed and undulated on its way down the window, passers-by could catch glimpses of the frenetic activity within. The heavy bass thump of the music could be heard outside the walls and at least a level below. A single, bulky door bot stood outside spouting the night's drink specials and admitting those who wished to enter.

The club's debut at the station had been something of a controversy. Station officials had denied the club's application on four different occasions, but thanks to a silent partner, it had eventually gone through. The partner, an unnamed interest from Earth, had cut through the red tape and bureaucracy to get the club its license. To this day, the club owners and key members of the station were the only people who knew the partner's identity. Many speculated that it was Hirohito Yutanni, owner of the largest technology corporation on Earth. Yutanni Flight Systems were the most prevalent computer systems in the UESA's fleet, and aboard private ships as well. It was even used on Europa and Neptune Stations. Why Yutanni had chosen to invest in a club on Europa was beyond anyone's guess, although it was rumored his teenage daughter frequented the station and she had somehow convinced her father to intervene. His daughter was a regular at the club, often there more than the actual owners were.

Jansen and Cody stood in front of the club staring at the front door. Still standing arm-in-arm, they looked like a young couple in love. Cody slowly turned to her crewmate and expressed a worried feeling with a single glance. This was not her place in the galaxy. She would often go out of her way to avoid crowds and heavily populated places. This was the last place she imagined herself, and yet, here she was. Looking at Jansen for some kind of reprieve, she saw him watching two scantily clad women dancing just inside the window bumping and grinding against each other.

Reaching up, she closed his gaping mouth and forcefully turned his attention to her. "Are you sure about this?"

"I have never been so sure about anything in my life," he assured her. "Wait," Cody said, turning them away from the door bot, "are you old enough to be in a place like this?"

Jansen nodded and lifted his right hand. Cody noticed the band-aid around his thumb for the first time. "I am tonight." He patted her on the back. "We'll talk inside."

Cody swallowed hard as she followed her companion to the door. "Okay." The door bot, a surly unit painted the same color as the walls, was from the same production line as TC-10. Special modifications had been made to his chassis to allow neon tubes to run over his body. The tubes alternated from red to gold and back again, looking as if illuminated, colored water was flowing through them. His single red eye fixed on the two. Lifting his bulky arm, he pressed it across the entrance, blocking their way. "Please submit to age verification," he instructed them in a low, deep, unemotional voice. A rectangular panel slid open on his chest revealing the touch pad and the club's rules. "By verifying your age, you also agree to adhere to the club's rules."

Cody raised her hand first. Pressing her thumb inside the small, blue rectangle on the screen, the rules quickly vanished, replaced with a waiting icon. After a few seconds, it vanished and was replaced by an image of two green, three-eyed aliens drinking and partying with several bikini-clad human women. "Welcome to Club Io" flashed above the animated image.

"Have fun in Club Io, and remember to drink responsibly," the door bot said, his voice now full of bounce. Turning his eye, he focused on Jansen. "Please submit to age verification. By verifying your—"

Jansen nodded. "I heard you the first time."

Lifting his bandaged thumb, he pressed it to the same rectangle Cody had. The same waiting icon appeared on the screen. Cody glanced at her companion nervously as the icon remained on the screen for what seemed an inordinate amount of time. Jansen remained cool and calm, completely sure of his plan. As the bot whirred and churned the information in front of them, he glanced over its shoulder into the club, trying to find the two nearly naked women he had spied earlier.

The image of the partying aliens reappeared on the screen. "Have fun in Club Io, and remember, drink responsibly," the door bot said finally.

Lowering his arm, he scooted to one side of the door allowing the young couple to pass.

Jansen and Cody moved through the door and stood in awe. Nearly dark, the club had been designed with numerous levels and platforms inside. Vaulted high above the bottom dance floor, the main ceiling contained the same image of Io that spun above the outer door. Stairs and escalators led to the various levels in the club, and each wound around the next. The same neon tubing that ran through the door bot outside wound throughout the club giving everything an orange glow. Music pulsed and thumped around the men and women packed into every corner. Glancing up through the place, Jansen spotted the bar on the third level. Grabbing Cody by the hand, he led her to the first escalator and started up.

Cody tapped Jansen on the shoulder. Leaning close, she shouted above the music. "You're only twenty, right?"

Jansen nodded with a mischievous smile. Lifting his right hand, he carefully peeled off one edge of the flesh-colored band-aid and showed Cody. There, attached to the rectangular piece of gauze, was a small, circular chip.

"How did you get one of those?" Cody stared at the object. She had only seen one other I-Chip before, the one programmed with her information and implanted in the flesh of her right thumb. The I-Chip not only contained one's personal information such as date of birth, government ID number and blood type, it was also used as a method of payment. The larger banks had realized by encoding it with a person's account information, they would always have their money with them. It was one part convenience; three parts advance marketing research the banks could sell to any company in the world. The microprocessor sent out a small signal capable of being picked up by base stations installed practically everywhere, or through the use of datapads. To be in the possession of an illegal I-Chip was a serious crime, punishable by exile to the Venusian penal colony. The government did not take this type of fraud lightly.

Jansen smiled. "Best not to ask." Wrapping the band-aid back across his finger, he pulled Cody around the corner and onto the next escalator.

As the lift slowly took them up to the third level bar, they watched all the people move and interact through the club. Every slice of life, from the young and beautiful to the old, was represented here at Club Io. They couldn't understand why protests had broken out over this place. It seemed like the perfect draw for the station, and would help increase business in all shops and restaurants. As Cody turned and peered into a darkened corner of the third level, she suddenly understood. There, seated amidst a table of at least ten others who were drinking and laughing, a man and woman were openly having sex.

Cody quickly averted her eyes, but found she wanted to look back. Turning to Jansen, she placed a hand on his shoulder. "I want to go back to my room."

"Come on," he protested, "we just got here."

Pointing over her shoulder, she hid her face in Jansen's chest.

Jansen looked over to see the couple in the corner. Turning back to Cody, he smiled and patted her back. "This is a great club!"

Cody laughed despite her discomfort.

Reaching the third level, Jansen led Cody to the bar. Grabbing two empty seats, they sat down and signaled one of the two bar bots. The top of the bar was made of the same neon substance as the tubes. The glass top washed from orange to red as the patrons set their glasses on it. The bar was packed with people laughing, dancing and trying their best to have a conversation above the music.

The first bar bot rolled in front of Jansen and Cody. Placing all four of its appendages on the bar, it leaned close to the two. "What can I do for you?"

Jansen leaned closer to the bar bot. "I want to get drunk."

The bar bot nodded. "Then you've come to the right place. Might I suggest the house specialty?"

"What is it?" Jansen asked.

"We like to call it the Europan Blizzard," the bar bot said proudly. "It's a blend of over seven different types of alcohol with a little citrus extract and coconut for texture and color."

Jansen nodded and held up two fingers.

The bot immediately grabbed two huge glasses from below the bar and set them in front of Jansen and Cody. Holding his fingers over the glass, liquor began to flow out. As the substances began to mix, the bar bot snatched a handful of coconut and tossed it in. Adding a final slice of lime floating on the top, he presented the drinks to Jansen and Cody. Quickly paying for them, Jansen leaned down and watched the coconut floating down through the clear alcohol, looking much like a snow globe. Lifting the glass, Jansen took a long drink of the concoction.

"What does it taste like?" Cody asked.

"I think after two or three sips of this," Jansen took another sip and swallowed it down, "it won't matter anymore."

Bravely lifting her glass, Cody stared at the clear liquid. Tipping it back to her lips, she took a quick taste and smiled. "It's not that bad." Glancing down the bar, she spotted an empty privacy booth at the far end of the platform. "Come on."

Grabbing Jansen's arm, the two wound through the busy platform until they reached the booth. With a singular curved seat and table in the center, the two slid in. Activating the privacy controls in the center of the table, the throbbing music and roar of the crowd quickly died out as the sound dampeners went into effect. As the silence surrounded them, Cody took a slow breath for the first time since entering the club. Giving herself a moment to adjust to the quiet, she took another sip of her drink.

"This is much better," she said at last.

Lifting his glass, he tapped it to Cody's. "Agreed."

"Do you feel better yet?"

"What?"

Cody smiled. "Not so bored anymore?"

Jansen nodded. "This is great. Thanks for coming with me."

"Anytime, Nugget."

"So where are you from, Lieutenant?"

Cody stirred her drink with a small straw. "New London."

"The Mars colony?" the young man asked surprised. Cody nodded. "The very same. You?"

Jansen shrugged. "Nowhere as exciting as that. Born and raised in Iowa."

"Why is that boring?" Cody asked curiously.

"It seemed growing up that everywhere else was advancing so much, technology-wise," he said as a far-off look appeared in his eye. "Iowa just wasn't that exciting. Most of the farmers there still cling to ancient traditions on growing and bringing in their crops. They still use hover-tractors there, for Christ's sake. They could have upgraded to harvesters long ago and cut nearly three-quarters of the work out of farming."

"That doesn't sound so bad," Cody commented. "Kind of peaceful."

"Sure, someone from New London would say that. You didn't have to live there."

"At least you could go outside and breathe fresh air," Cody shot back. "Try living under a dome all your young life when every commercial you watch is of some kids frolicking on the beach and all you see when you look out your window is the same barren, rust red landscape."

The two sat in an uncomfortable silence for a long time. They had only been working together for nearly four weeks now and had yet to get to know each other. They had talked before, but in a social setting with Kira, Chris and Captain Hull in attendance. They had never really had the opportunity, or inclination, to spend time alone together. Cody suddenly began to silently question his motives. Here they were, alone, drinking at a bar. Sitting back in the booth, she tried to scoot slightly away from Jansen, without making it look like that was what she was trying to do. Setting her drink on the table, she placed her hand flat just beyond the privacy console. A small, red panic button was situated in the center of it.

"So," Cody said slowly, "What exactly did you have in mind for tonight?" Jansen returned his attention to Cody and shrugged. "I really didn't have any set plans," he admitted. "I just didn't want to be in that room by myself anymore."

"Aren't you bunking with the captain?"

"Supposed to be," Jansen corrected. "Saw him for about an hour this afternoon with some woman and he hasn't been back since."

"What woman?" Cody asked curiously. "What did she look like?"

"Tall, brunette," Jansen said, trying to remember. "She was in a UESA uniform. Didn't catch her rank."

"Did you see the patch on her sleeve?"

Jansen closed his eyes and thought for a moment. "I'm pretty sure it was one of the new Triumph class ships, but I can't remember which."

"The Armstrong?"

Jansen snapped his fingers. "That's it. How did you know?"

"Oh crap," Cody breathed.

"What?" Jansen urged, "What is it?"

"That was Captain Hull of the Armstrong," Cody said, taking another sip of her drink.

"Captain Hull?"

Cody nodded. "Our captain's ex-wife." She pushed her glass away and leaned close to the young ensign. "The captain received a wedding invitation from her about a week ago. I accidentally erased it," Cody admitted. "And when I say 'accidentally', I mean intentionally."

"Why?"

"You've never seen the captain around her. He gets all wishy-washy and weird. Trust me, it's better if he doesn't know."

"But it looks like she caught up with him," Jansen said, stating the obvious. "Is he going to be all right?"

Cody glanced outside the booth and shook her head. "Why don't you go ask him yourself?"

A curious expression crossed Jansen's face. Cody pointed across the bar. The young ensign turned to see his captain standing there with a drink in his hand. He looked almost broken in his wrinkled suit. Jumping up from the booth, Cody quickly crossed the platform and retrieved her captain. Bringing him back to the booth, both slid inside.

Cody placed her hand gently on his shoulder. "What are you doing here, Captain?"

Hull's face was long. The gray dress shirt he wore beneath his wrinkled black suit jacket was misbuttoned about halfway up and it looked like he had spilled something on it as well. His tie hung out of his lapel pocket and he was completely missing his socks. They had seen him look better. "Long night," he said after a minute.

"Want to talk about it, Skipper?" Jansen asked.

Hull looked up and stared at the young ensign. No one but Chris ever called him that. It sounded strange coming from someone else's mouth. He let it go. "Not really, but thanks. Just a few things I need to work through."

"We're good listeners." Cody smiled.

Hull reached over and patted Cody on the back and smiled at his navigator. "I know you are, but really, I'm okay." An odd look crossed his face, "A more important question is: what the hell are you doing here, Katrina?"

Cody shrugged. "Jansen just wanted a little company. Thought I could expand my horizons a little."

Hull looked from Cody to Jansen. "You two have heard my policy on dating, right?"

Both nodded quickly like children being scolded.

"That's not it at all," Jansen urged. "I was awake and bored and asked Lieutenant Cody if she wanted to come down here for a drink. That's it."

"Okay," Hull said with a smirk on his face.

Hearing Jansen say it out loud made Cody feel slightly better as well.

"So this is a helluva place," Hull said, after taking another sip of his drink. "What made you two decide to come here?"

Cody produced the yellow flier from her pocket. "Good advertising." Hull nodded.

The three sat silently for a moment, nursing their respective drinks. The silence around them seemed deafening at the time. Finally, Hull reached over and tapped three buttons on the console in the center of the table. "Let's see what's on television."

Relieved, the two crewmen nodded.

A small screen rose from the table and locked into place. Hitting another button, he watched the screen flicker to life. The club's information channel was the first to display. A lovely young woman appeared to the side of the image giggling. Turning toward the screen, she waved hello.

"Welcome to Club Io," she cooed. "The hottest place in the solar system this side of the sun."

Jansen laughed at her horrible joke. Hull and Cody immediately glared at him. "What? It was kind of funny."

Shaking his head, Hull returned his attention to the monitor. He listened as the virtual greeter ran down a list of the club's activities and drink specials.

"Club Io is the future of dating!" she said proudly. "In each booth, we've installed cameras so you can meet the other clubbers without leaving your seat! Just hit the green button in the center of your console to activate the random camera, or input a specific three-digit number to directly dial another booth. You'll never leave the club alone again!" Her image disappeared from the screen and was replaced by the image of Io.

"Want to give it a shot?" Jansen asked.

Hull turned to his ensign. "What, the dating thing?"

"Yeah," Jansen said with a smile. "It seems kind of voyeuristic. We don't have to chat with anyone else, we can just scan the other booths to see what's going on."

"You've got some real issues, Ensign," Hull laughed. "I'm game. How about you, Lieutenant?"

Cody shrugged. "Sure."

Jensen activated the video system. The screen snapped to a bright blue with the word "searching…" emblazoned in white. After a few moments, the image flickered and showed the first booth. It was completely empty. Someone had accidentally left the video system on. Hitting the search button again, the screen was once again covered in blue. The image of three beautiful women suddenly appeared laughing and drinking.

"What took you guys so long?" They slowly turned to look at the video screen. "Hey," they said in dismay, "you're not our dates." Reaching over to the screen, they quickly terminated the link.

"Well this is going well," Hull said snidely. "I think you'd have better luck if you went out to the dance floor and randomly clubbed women on the head, Ensign."

Jansen shrugged. "One more try."

He hit the search button. As the service rotated through active camera feeds, it chose one at random. The image of a darkened booth appeared. Three men were seated on the curved seat talking quietly. They had apparently not seen the video screen's activation.

Hull looked at the image. "Isn't that Station Chief Ramirez?"

Cody leaned close to the monitor and squinted her eyes. "I think so. Who are those two men he's with? One of them looks familiar."

Hull nodded. "He does. Can't quite place him though. Anyone mind if I say hello? Chief Ramirez is an old buddy of mine. I haven't had the time to stop by his office since we've arrived."

Jansen and Cody shrugged. Reaching over, Jansen activated the audio on the video feed. They could instantly hear the conversation of the three men.

"…Wants to take the artifact."

Hull recognized the voice of Ramirez. He started to say something, but a second voice cut him off.

"The Vice President needs to be eliminated if he gets in our way," the voice said ominously.

Hull quickly tore off his jacket and draped it over the video screen. Cody looked curiously at her captain. "We can't let them see us," he whispered.

"The artifact is too important to us to let them take it. We have to make sure it's in our hands."

"I will not be a part of his cover-up," Ramirez said to the other men, "but I don't want to be a party to killing either. If we eliminate the Vice President, the investigation will run too deep. I don't think any of us can avoid that."

Hull, Cody and Jansen sat in awe in their booth listening to the plot unfolding somewhere in the club. They couldn't believe their ears. Hull's gut reaction was to warn the Vice President, but he needed more information than just three men sitting in a bar talking. Holding his wristcomm to the speaker, he tapped the memo button and began recording. Pulling a small pad out of his pocket, Jansen tried to hack into the signal. After a few moments, he had gained access to their booth's camera and was recording the feed as well. He started to triangulate their position.

"You're just full of illegal equipment tonight," Cody whispered in Jansen's ear.

"We have already been authorized to use whatever force is necessary," the second man warned. "We will not let the government pull the wool over the public's eyes any longer."

"I agree," Ramirez stated again, this time more emphatically, "but we cannot kill the Vice President of Earth! That's going too far!"

The second man in the booth pulled a pulse pistol from his jacket and grabbed Ramirez by the collar of his uniform. "I should kill you where you sit for disobeying orders," the man growled.

The third man threw himself forward and yanked the gun from the second man's hand. "No! This isn't our way!"

"Can I get you folks anything else?"

Hull, Jansen, and Cody looked up with a start at the waitress who had entered their booth unnoticed. Hull bolted up from the booth and pulled her outside the privacy bubble with a start.

"Did you hear that?"

Jansen hovered his finger over the button that would end the transmission link.

"I think we're being monitored. Scan for tracers."

"Our video screen," Ramirez said quickly, "it's been activated."

Jansen killed the feed and snapped off his pad. "We need to go. Now."

Pushing Cody out of the booth, he tapped Hull on the shoulder as they moved into the crowd.

Hull smiled at the startled waitress as he pushed past her to leave. "We're fine. Thank you!"

Spotting Ramirez as they headed down the second escalator, Hull's crew tried to act casually. They hadn't been made, and Jansen had killed his tracer before they had a chance to track it. Hull glanced over the railing at the two men standing next to the station chief. A spark of recognition burned in his mind like a glowing ember, but he still couldn't put his finger on where he'd seen the man before. He watched the three men split up and start to search the club. All three looked to be holding a weapon under their jackets.

Hitting the first floor, Hull led his crewmates toward the front door. Once outside, he quickly turned the corner and headed for the Dionysus.

Putting some distance between them and the club, Hull finally stopped. "I want you to contact Chris and TC," he said to Cody. "Tell them we'll all be arriving at the ship in twenty minutes."

Cody nodded and began to activate her wristcomm.

Hull turned to Jansen. "Get Kira and meet us on the ship."

"And you, Captain?" Jansen asked quickly.

Hull smiled wryly. "I'll meet you on the Tereshkova shortly."

CHAPTER EIGHT

The door slid open causing the lights to flicker on. Glancing quickly around the room, he spotted his target. Stepping inside, he kept his hand firmly on the grip of the pulse pistol concealed in his jacket. Walking carefully across the floor, he quickly killed the lights on the console located on the far wall. The room was thrust back into darkness with only the lights above the hospital beds and in the intensive care unit casting a soft blue glow on the floor. Stepping carefully over the legs of two patients who had fallen asleep in each other's arms, he turned his head and stopped.

There, asleep on a thin cot just inside the door was Dr. Sumner. Turning, he admired her beauty. He had been keeping a watchful eye on her ever since her arrival almost six months ago. She was the perfect woman in his opinion: brilliant and beautiful. It was too bad they didn't have more time. They could have had something special. He stopped and scolded himself. He hadn't done anything in the six months she had been here, what made him think he would do anything with more time? He was being facetious. There was nothing there, nor would there ever be. All he could do was admire her from afar. He could tell himself that their UESA ranks kept them apart, that it wasn't appropriate for her to date a superior, but in reality, it was his innate fear of rejection that kept them apart. Now she had signed her own death certificate. It was only a matter of time before he did to her what he had done to the rest of those "exposed".

Turning away from Julie, he walked across the room and stood next to the massive IC unit. Placing his hand on the transparasteel cover, he leaned over and flipped open the access console. Checking to ensure the regimen of drugs to keep the patient's mental acuities subdued was still working, he nodded. He hated to do this, as he knew the man well. He had been to several functions and played virtual golf with him. He was losing a good friend today, but the cause was more important. At least that's what they told him. He had to be a good soldier— after all, they were the ones who had placed him in this position. If he wanted to retain this job, he had to follow orders. He knew he could wait a few days for the drugs in the archaeologist's system to overwhelm him and take his life, but by that point, a full investigation would be underway. No evidence could remain. Not even one of his dearest friends on the station.

Lifting a hypospray out of his jacket pocket, he snapped open another access panel. Keying in his personal code, he watched a small cylinder extend toward him. Pressing the barrel of the hypospray to the flesh like substance that covered the cylinder, he emptied the contents of it inside. Hitting another sequence of keys, he watched the maroon-colored liquid empty from the cylinder into the IC unit. Snapping the two panels shut, he peered into the transparasteel cover. The various tubes feeding the drugs into the archaeologist shifted from their normal clear color to a dark red resembling blood. As the first of the chemical entered the archaeologist's body, he started to convulse. His assassin quickly dropped the hypospray back into his pocket and charged toward the door. The archaeologist would be dead in a matter of seconds and there wasn't anything that could save him now.

Running through the door, he slapped the emergency close button on the opposite side, slamming it shut just as alarms began to sound in the IC unit. Locking the access again, he fell back against the wall and took a deep breath. Lifting his head, he stared into the bright lights installed into the ceiling. There was no time to waste. He had to get out of here. The Vice President had probably installed warning devices on the IC unit to alert him to any change in the patient's condition. It was only through an insider that he even knew the location of the patients. Dropping the hypospray into a nearby trash bin recessed into the wall, he keyed his security override into the small panel above it. He watched as the bin emptied its contents into the compactor below. Quickly saying a silent goodbye to his friend, Chief Ramirez vanished down the halls of Europa Station.

***

As soon as the door slammed shut, Julie was off her cot. Rushing toward the IC unit, she pressed her palms flat on the transparasteel and stared inside. The usually clear tubes now flowed blood red. As the alarms tied to his vital signs began to sound, she watched his body convulse in the unit. She turned to see Jim and the nurses standing around her.

"Can you do anything?" Julie asked breathlessly. Jim and the nurses remained quiet.

"Anything?" Julie asked again.

Sue looked at the other nurses, then back to Julie. Stepping forward, she gently pushed Julie out of the way. Clicking open the access panels on the side of the unit, she glanced up at the convulsing man inside. There was only one course of action available to her. Keying in the universal access code, she watched the red “locked” light behind the keypad shift to green. Sue turned to the rest of the prisoners. “There’s only one thing we can do. Code 1104.”

One of the nurses gasped and covered her mouth.

Julie and Jim looked inquisitively at Sue. “What the hell is Code 1104?” Julie asked quickly.

“Every IC unit has a special code built into it for this kind of situation,” Sue said evenly, still keeping an eye on the convulsing man behind her. “It releases a lethal dose of chemicals into the patient’s body that kill them almost instantly and painlessly.”

“That’s it?” Julie screamed, “You want to kill him?”

“He’s dying already,” Sue shot back.

“We don’t know that,” Jim argued. “He could just be having a seizure. We should wait. Help is bound to come. Someone has to be monitoring these alarms.”

“There’s no time!” Sue pointed to the archaeologist’s face. “He’s in pain! Look at him!”

The archaeologist’s head snapped forward and impacted against the transparasteel with a crunch. Everyone jumped back with a start. As he fell back, a splatter of blood remained on the surface and on his forehead just above his right eye. His body continued to convulse as blood ran down from the cut into his already battered and bruised eyes.

"I'm not waiting any longer!" Sue yelled. "This man is suffering. I can end that." She started to reach for the keypad.

"Step away from the IC unit."

Everyone in the room spun around to see two men in black EV suits standing with their weapons drawn. "Stand away from the IC unit, or I will be forced to fire," the first man warned again.

Sue gritted her teeth. She was tired of this place, and of being a prisoner. She was going to do her job, no matter what the consequences. She was going to end this man's suffering. Leaning over quickly, she started to tap in the code.

Without hesitation, both men squeezed the triggers on their pulse pistols. The weapons simultaneously discharged a single pulse of plasma that burned gold as it exited the end of the barrel. Moving across the room at nearly double the speed of a traditional bullet, the plasma pulses hit Sue in the side and back instantly tearing into her. As they continued through her body, they charred and seared every bit of tissue, muscle and bone they came in contact with. Sue snapped straight up as the pain surged through her body like a lightning bolt. Falling back to the ground, her body crumpled lifelessly into a heap. She was dead and the whole ordeal had taken less than a second.

His pistol cradled in his hands, one of the soldiers moved through the crowd of patients toward the IC unit while the second trooper kept his weapon at the ready. Glancing at the digital display above the keypad, he saw the nurse had entered three digits of the command. Another millisecond, and she would have completed the sequence. Turning back to the other trooper, the first one nodded.

Lifting his arm, the second trooper keyed the mic built into his helmet. “We’re clear, doctor. You can enter now.”

The door to the containment room slid open again. Julie turned to see Quentin enter the room with another trooper at his side. Pushing through the crowd of startled and scared people, Quentin headed straight for the IC unit. Canceling the sequence the nurse had been trying to input, he quickly entered his access code. The keys once again lit green. Snapping open the second panel, he dropped the silver briefcase he was carrying on top of the transparasteel. Hurriedly flipping it open, he ran over the available medicines and compounds it contained. Selecting the most potent sedative he had, he snapped the small, round bottle into a hypospray he had also removed from the case. Typing in a code on the second keypad, he waited for the small cylinder to extend. Looking at the convulsing archaeologist, he saw the last few drops of a red substance in his feeder tubes empty into his system. With a curious look on his face, Quentin pressed the hypo spray to the cylinder and injected the sedative. The archaeologist convulsed one final time and stopped. “You did it, doctor,” one of the nurses said from behind.

Quentin quickly waved them off. Staring into the IC unit, he watched the first of the sedative appear in the feeder tubes. He hadn’t done anything. Grabbing his personal pad from his pocket, he snapped it into the waiting socket on the access panel. Quickly, he pressed the download button. As a small green light appeared on his pad, he ripped it from the socket and began to cycle through the information displayed. His eyes widened. Saving the file, he powered down the pad and dropped it into his pocket. Turning, Quentin headed for the door.

"How's the patient, doctor?" one of the troopers asked. "He's dead," Quentin replied as he headed out the door.

The three troopers turned and stared at each other. Turning, they followed Quentin.

Once outside, Quentin started down the hallway, mumbling something. "Doctor?" one of the troopers called after him. Shaking his helmet, he holstered his weapon and charged down the hallway. Reaching out, he grabbed Quentin by the shoulder, forcefully stopped him. "You want to tell me what the hell is going on, Doctor?"

"That's exactly what I would like to know," Quentin said quickly.

***

TC activated the airlock to the Tereshkova. Standing back, he watched Jansen, Cody and Kira join Chris inside the zero-gravity environment.

Kira looked at Chris, who was sipping a cup of steaming coffee through a straw. "Don't you ever sleep?"

Chris shook his head. "Repairs have to get done."

TC turned to his crewmates. "Would someone mind telling me what the hell is going on?"

Kira shrugged. "I'm in the dark as well, TC." She turned to Jansen, who had awakened her from a perfectly good dream. "Are you going to fill us in?"

Jansen looked nervously to Cody, then back to the others. "We should probably wait for the captain."

"Why?" Chris asked.

"This is very important," Cody stated quickly. "I don't think we should start without him."

Kira keyed off the nervousness in Cody's voice. "I don't like this." The airlock chime startled the crew. Turning back to the door, TC activated the controls. Through the door, Hull and Jennifer floated inside. Hull was still in his gray shirt and slacks, while Jennifer was in her uniform. Hull nodded for TC to close the door again. Once inside, the captain addressed his crew.

"This is Captain Hull of the Armstrong," Hull introduced them. "I've asked her to join us because we could use all the help we can get."

"Hello, Jenny," Chris said smugly, instantly recognizing the captain's old flame. He thought he had seen the last of her.

"Chris, you old bastard," Jennifer replied in the same tone as Chris, "You're still alive?"

Chris started to snap back, but a quick glance from the captain silenced him. "Ensign Jensen, Lieutenant Cody and I have come across some very disturbing news," he said slowly. "Jensen, will you play the tape?"

Jensen nodded. Spinning, he grabbed the wall and pulled himself in. Pulling his tracer from his pocket, he interfaced it with the door console. Routing the feed into the two screens on the far side of the room, he played the recording he had made earlier in the evening. The crew watched the video in astonished silence. After the roughly thirty-five seconds of video ended, Hull turned and instructed Jansen to play it again. The second time through didn't lessen the impact on anyone. Jennifer reached over and placed her hand on Hull's shoulder.

As the video ended for the second time, the captain turned and looked into the faces of his crew. "Chief Ramirez and his co-conspirators are obviously planning to assassinate the Vice President," he said calmly. "We could be the only ones who know."

Kira looked around at her shipmates. "What do we do?"

"I think it's obvious," Chris replied. "We take this evidence directly to the Vice President."

"If a group suddenly shows up at the Vice President's door, the assassins could get nervous and step up their attempt," Kira argued.

"She's right," Hull said quickly. "We need to be smart about this, and we need to move quickly." He looked down at his watch. "It's nearly five in the morning now," he took a deep breath, "Jansen, I think it's best if you and I go alone. Too many people showing up at once will arouse suspicion."

"We don't even know where the Vice President is staying in the station," Jennifer pointed out, "and I don't think Chief Ramirez is going to help us out."

Hull turned to Jansen. "Can you find out?"

Jansen nodded. "It'll take a few minutes. I'll have to access the station's computer through our own. There's a lot of encryption there."

"Jansen, you little devil," Kira smiled. "You're a slicer?"

Hull smiled. “Our little ensign is just full of surprises tonight.” He turned back to his crew. “I want all of you down at the Dionysus in case of emergency. You’ll be close enough to help should the need arise. TC,” he turned to the big bot, “I need you to stay with the Tereshkova. I want you to start prepping for launch.”

The big bot nodded. “I’ll have the engines warm for you, Captain.”

“Chris,” he turned to his engineer, “can you smuggle a few pulse pistols into the station?”

Chris thought for a moment. “It’ll be tough to get ‘em through the Dock Master’s security, Skipper, but if anyone can do it, I can.” Hull patted his friend on the shoulder.

“I have it, Captain,” Jansen announced.

Turning, Hull looked at the ensign. “Where is he?”

“The Vice President is staying in the Ambassadorial Suite,” he scrolled down through the information on his tracer, “in pod three, alpha section.”

Hull nodded and turned to Jennifer. “I want you to stay with me.”

“Should I alert my command staff?” Jennifer asked.

Hull chewed on the request for a moment and finally shook his head. “I don’t think so. We need to keep the loop as small as possible right now.” He placed his hands on Jennifer’s shoulders. After the scene earlier in her room, he never thought he would see her again. “I’m sure your crew is trustworthy, but we need to keep a lid on this.”

Jennifer nodded.

"We all have our assignments," Hull said finally. "Keep your wristcomms open, and let's go to work."

CHAPTER NINE

The alarm clock next to his bed began to squawk, waking him from a dead sleep. He had only gotten to bed a few hours before and desperately needed more sleep. Rolling onto his side, he stared at the large, red digital numbers. He contemplated hitting the snooze button for a moment, but his sense of duty compelled him to sit up. Propping himself against the headboard, the Vice President extended his arms wide and stretched. As he flexed his tired muscles, a yawn welled up from deep inside his chest and forced its way out of his mouth.

Twisting his feet over the edge of the bed, he craned his neck to the right and then to the left. It crackled and popped in protest. Leaning forward, he rubbed the sleep out of his eyes with the heels of his palms. Standing up, he glanced at the clock one more time. It was just after five in the morning. Grabbing his silk robe from the foot of his bed, he tried to pull it on but kept missing the left sleeve in his exhaustion. Finally hitting the hole, he wrapped the robe tightly around his powder blue pajamas and tied the belt over his stomach. Slipping on his gray plush slippers, he yawned again.

"Lights," he said groggily. "Slowly," he specified.

The lights in his suite began to rise. As his eyes adjusted, he stumbled to the main door. He could see light spilling in from beneath. His security team was obviously already awake and moving about. As the lights in his room finally reached maximum brightness, he pressed his hand to the console next to the door and activated it. As it slid open, two men in dark suits, one reading the morning e-paper and the other working in the small kitchenette, greeted him. He could smell the aroma of coffee brewing and instantly craved the steaming hot liquid. Moving into the kitchenette, he snatched the e-paper from his security guard and grabbed a coffee mug from the counter.

Handing the mug to his second guard, he leaned back against the countertop and began to peruse the morning's news stored in the black datapad. The electronic paper was known as the Europa Herald Times, and was little more than a collection of stories culled from news services. It held one or two small entries regarding the station and the monthly lunch calendar, but that was about it for local content. Wyman couldn't imagine the paper's staff consisting of more than two or three people at most. It probably didn't take them long each morning to scan the headlines off the wire and paste them into the Herald Times. Hell, one person could probably achieve that. They didn't even need a staff.

Tossing the pad back to his security guard, he accepted the steaming hot mug of coffee from the other. Lifting it to his nose, he took a hearty sniff of the liquid. Glancing down into the light brown colored beverage, he knew his guard remembered how he took it. Taking a small sip of it, he nodded approvingly at the man. Cradling the warm mug in his hands, he hovered over it like a man first discovering the warmth of fire. Taking another sip, he began to feel the caffeine hit his blood stream. He had no idea how some people survived without this life- giving beverage. He realized he was drinking more than just the regular canned variety. Wyman looked up at his guard. "Special blend?"

The guard nodded with a smile, happy the Vice President had noticed. "From my personal stash, sir."

Wyman reached over and patted the well-built man on the back. "What's your name, son?"

"Terrell, Mr. Vice President," the guard said proudly. "Ansil Terrell."

"Well, Ansil, you just got yourself a raise," Wyman said with a smile. "On one condition."

"Yes, sir?"

"Make this special blend of yours every morning." Wyman took another sip of the coffee. "Deal?"

Ansil smiled and nodded. "Yes, sir."

Wyman headed back for his room to hit the shower. As he walked by his other security guard, he smacked him on the shoulder. "Don't steal my morning paper, Gordon."

"Sorry, sir," Gordon responded hastily.

As Wyman disappeared behind his bedroom door, Gordon stood up and stared at Ansil. The elder of the two guards on duty, Gordon sneered at the younger man. "Kiss ass."

"What?" Ansil asked. "What did I do?"

"It's from my personal stash," Gordon said mockingly. Ansil looked confused. "But it is."

Gordon blew Ansil off and retreated to the opposite side of the living room. Dropping down into the plush black couch, he snapped on his datapad and began to read through the paper again. Kicking his feet up onto the coffee table in front of him, he knew it would be at least half an hour before the Vice President emerged from the bathroom. He had plenty of time to rest up before the six o'clock meeting with Commander Trudeau.

The door chime startled both guards.

Leaping up from the couch, Gordon sprinted across the floor and slammed his back up against the doorframe. He watched Ansil cross out of the kitchenette and take up position on the opposite side of the door. Both men drew their pulse pistols from the holsters inside their jackets. Gripping their weapons tightly, both men nodded to signal their readiness.

Gordon slowly reached over his shoulder and activated the intercom. "Who's there?"

"It's Captain Alexander Hull from the Tereshkova. It's urgent I speak to the Vice President."

"The Vice President isn't taking visitors right now," Gordon announced quickly.

"Please," Hull persuaded, "It's a matter of government security. I have reason to believe there is going to be an assassination attempt on the Vice President's life."

Gordon glanced to Ansil nervously, then to the video screen. "Hold your UESA ID to the camera outside the door," Gordon instructed Hull. Turning fully, he activated the view screen on the control pad. He instantly recognized the captain and the member of his command crew. He waited for Hull to hold up ID.

"Thank you," Gordon said. "Please step back from the door." Gordon panned the camera up and down the hallway to ensure the two men were alone. Once satisfied, he signaled for Ansil to remain ready. He holstered his weapon and unlocked the door. "Please step inside and raise your arms," Gordon instructed them.

Hull, Jennifer, and Jansen slowly complied. As they moved inside, the guard closed and locked the door again. Pulling a cylindrical wand from his coat, Gordon snapped it open, instantly tripling its length. He activated the device and began to run it over the three. Once satisfied they were clean, he snapped it closed and deposited it back into his jacket. Turning, he motioned for the trio to have a seat on the couch. As they crossed the floor and sat down, Gordon and Ansil moved carefully behind them. Grabbing a chair from the kitchenette, Gordon pulled it across the room and sat down opposite. Meanwhile, Ansil hovered in the background with his weapon at the ready.

"What the hell is this about an assassination attempt?" Gordon asked pointedly.

"We seem to have stumbled onto it by accident," Hull replied. He nodded to Jansen. "Ensign Jansen was able to catch thirty-five seconds of the conversation we overheard. In the video, we can clearly identify Station Chief Ramirez, but we have no idea who the other two men are or what they're talking about."

Jansen pressed play on his tracer and quickly handed it to Gordon. The senior guard watched the video grimly. After it ended, he tapped the play button again. He looked up at Hull and handed the tracer back. "I need a copy of this right now."

Hull nodded. He watched his ensign retrieve a micro-CD from his pocket and insert it into the tracer. In a matter of seconds, the burn was complete. Ejecting the CD, Jansen handed it to Gordon.

"What do you think?" Hull asked finally.

"It scares the hell out of me," Gordon admitted. "But there are a couple things I didn't hear on that video that scare me even more."

"Such as?" Jennifer inquired.

"Such as who these men are working for, and more importantly, a time frame for the assassination attempt," Gordon admitted. "It could come at any time, from anywhere."

"What the hell is this artifact they keep referring to on the video?" Hull queried.

"That's classified," Gordon replied gruffly. He turned to Ansil. "Please alert the Vice President that we need his attention."

***

Digging her fingernails into the tiny space between the console and the wall, she yanked firmly down. Her nails cracked and snapped off. Cursing under her breath, she pulled her hands away shaking them to try and lessen the pain. Turning to the others, Julie shrugged. "I don't see any of you coming up with any ideas."

Jim crossed the room toward the console. Reaching into his pocket, he produced a small, flat, circular piece of metal. Stepping past Julie, he dug the edge of the object in between the console and the wall. "My mother gave me this as a good luck charm," he said as he wiggled the object into position. "It used to be a penny," he said with a grunt, "but it was flattened on some kind of tracks." He pressed the thin edge of the copper disc firmly inside the crack. "I don't really know much about it, except that it used to be a kind of currency used on Earth." Holding both his thumbs on the bottom of the flattened penny, he pushed up with all his strength. He heard the seal between the console and wall begin to give way. "It's been passed down through my family for over three hundred and fifty years now," he said finally as the console broke free of the wall. "And it's always brought me good luck." Smiling at the others, he grabbed the exposed edge of the console and pulled it open.

Julie smiled and patted Jim on the back. Stepping around him, she peered into the exposed wires and circuitry. "You wouldn't happen to have some kind of magic coin that can hotwire doors in your other pocket, would you?"

Jim flipped the flattened penny with his thumb and shook his head. "That represented the extent of my usefulness in this situation," he said. "I'm a biologist, not an engineer."

Julie looked to the other two women in the room. Without hesitation, each shook their head. With a sigh, she turned back to the mess of wires before her. "I'll give it a shot. Maybe I can mess it up bad enough so they can't get back in again. If I'm lucky."

Jim reached out and handed the flattened penny to Julie. As she accepted the offer, she smiled. "Thanks." Dropping it into her pocket, she placed her hands cautiously on the edge of the panel. It was still coursing with electricity. One wrong connection or touch, and she could be in trouble. Grabbing the nearest two wires, she ripped them from the board and began to randomly touch them to other circuits.

"We're not going to get out of here, are we?" One of the nurses had started to pace nervously behind the others. Turning, she stared at Sue's body, still on the floor where she had fallen earlier. Two dark burn marks were visible in the back of her nurse uniform around the charred flesh where she had been hit with the pulses. "I don't want to end up like Sue."

Jim turned and looked at the frightened young woman. "We're gonna get out of here. We have to keep our wits about us." He paused. "We can't start panicking."

A shower of sparks erupted from the console. Julie leapt back with a grunt, just barely missing the brunt of the electricity. Shaking her head, she moved back to the console and waved away some of the acrid smoke that had settled around it.

"Yeah?" The nurse stared at Jim with a half-crazed look in her eyes. "I don't think we have a lot of options. We're going to stay here and die. They're going to come back in and pick us off one by one. What are the chances that she's going to get that door open?"

Alarms suddenly began to blare in the room. Each head in the room snapped around to face Julie.

She stood there with a cocky smile on her face. "I think we should run now." She pointed to the open door behind her.

Jim charged up and took Julie into a bear hug. "I could kiss you."

Julie broke free of the embrace and turned toward the door. "Not before some mouthwash, mister." Grabbing Jim's hand, she charged out into the hallway. Red sirens were churning overhead and the sound of alarms echoed out from the containment room. "Go," Julie commanded the nurses. "You two will blend in easier than Jim or me. Don't look back. Just get out of here."

The two nurses nodded. With one final look, they each charged off in different directions.

"What about us?" Jim asked warily as the two started down the corridor. Julie slid her hand into his. "We're getting off this station. I don't know how, but we have to find a way to stop them. I want to expose these bastards for what they really are."

Jim laced his fingers through hers and nodded. "I'm in."

The warmth of his hand was comforting to her. She slowly looked up into his rich brown eyes. "Let's go."

Julie felt a knot forming deep in her stomach as she ran. Glancing back over her shoulder at the empty hall behind her, she furrowed her brow. Who was she going to tell? If the station chief and Vice President were in on this, she was running out of options. Add that to the fact she was roughly two hundred and twenty-four million miles from Earth, and she had a major problem on her hands. Escape at this point was improbable. There had to be a way.

***

Trudeau barked orders at his men as he checked his watch. It was nearly six in the morning. The Vice President would be arriving any moment and he was missing one soldier.

He glanced worriedly around the Wet Lab. Divided into two sections, the first was designed for individual divers and easily portable equipment while the second half contained the main submersion pool. Several sleek, white submersible vehicles were above the main pool. The water in the Wet Lab seemed to have a luminous quality about it as it sat silently in the perfectly pressurized room. Huge banks of lights were installed just below the surface of the pools throwing light down on the muddy surface of the moon. Sometimes members of the biology division would come down and just sit beside the submersion pool and watch the water hoping to catch an elusive glimpse of life. To Trudeau, it wasn't quite as elusive. He thought back to the image of the artifact in his mind. It was staggering to him that such an object could even exist. He had never stopped and considered the possibility of life beyond the third planet of his solar system. To him, that was enough.

His three men in their dark EV suits worked around several piles of equipment. He had gathered everything the President had asked for on this mission, including the most high-powered stasis field man had ever produced. He had no idea, nor did the President's top advisors, what caused the first research team who found the artifact to act as they did. It obviously wasn't biological as the station's doctor had proven, but it was something. They had to be prepared for anything.

Dropping down to his knees, he snapped the clasp closed on his boot buckle. Making sure the seam between his suit and boots was secure, he stood and lifted his helmet off a nearby stand. Reaching down, he tapped several buttons on the main control panel of his matching black EV suit. Testing the status of the suit, he ran through several diagnostic programs. The suits had been specially designed to withstand the crushing pressures of the Europan ocean and still be as light and mobile as any other EV suit. These were very nearly like the ones used by the research team, but also contained extra shielding within their layers and a personal electromagnetic shield that should protect the men from any harmful effects emanating from the artifact. Reaching down, he made sure his pulse pistol was securely holstered.

The hiss of a nearby door caught his attention. Looking up, he saw his fourth soldier running into the room trying to snap the helmet of his EV suit in place. Dropping his helmet on a table, Trudeau marched across the room and caught the soldier before he could meet up with the rest of his squad. "Do we have a problem, soldier?"

The fourth soldier immediately snapped to attention. "Sir, no, sir!"

"You're nearly twenty-five minutes late to your post," Trudeau growled.

"Do you have an explanation for this?"

"Sir, I was trying to requisition a piece of equipment, sir."

Trudeau began to circle the soldier slowly, much like a shark waiting for its prey to bleed to death. "And what is this mysterious piece of equipment absolutely vital to the success of this mission?"

"Sir, replacement computer coil for my EV suit, sir."

"Are you incompetent, soldier?"

The fourth soldier didn't know how to reply. "Sir, no, sir!"

"Well you must be to have to replace a computer coil right before your duty begins," Trudeau barked. "Under standard Ministry of Defense procedure, all equipment must be checked the day before a mission. Any units even suspected of being faulty must be replaced then and there. Why is that, soldier?"

"Sir, because we are only as good as our equipment, sir!"

"That's right, soldier," Trudeau growled. "What would happen if you were out in the middle of the Europan ocean and your computer coil failed?"

"Sir, I would die, sir. My environmental controls would fail to operate and I would asphyxiate, sir."

Trudeau allowed the man to think about his statement for a moment. "Do we have the problem fixed, soldier?"

"Sir, yes, sir!"

"Then get to work!" Trudeau screamed in the soldier's face.

"Sir, yes, sir!" The fourth soldier snapped from attention and charged across the Wet Lab toward his comrades. Lifting his arm, he tapped several buttons on his wrist computer. The rectangular screen blinked to life and showed him the status of his newly installed core. The special alterations he had made to the device were communicating beautifully with the other modifications he had made to his suit. It was too bad none of them would be around after today, he told himself. They were a work of sheer brilliance. Hitting a final button on his wrist, a small display appeared on the inside of his visor giving him the status of his modifications. He made one final check to make sure all was ready. He joined the other three soldiers just as the door hissed open again.

"Good morning, Admiral," Trudeau snapped to attention and greeted the Vice President.

The Vice President walked slowly into the room, his white uniform from the day before replaced by the same dark blue jumpsuit every member of the UESA wore. His two guards, Gordon and Ansil, were also dressed in dark blue jumpsuits. They flanked the Vice President on either side and appeared to be even more alert than usual, their hands on the pulse pistols hidden just inside their jumpsuits. Following the Vice President and his guards was Hull, Jennifer, and Jansen. Hull kept his vision trained on the Vice President while Jansen worked the small tracer in his hand.

"Commander," Wyman returned the greeting. "How go the preparations?"

"Everything is in order, sir," Trudeau assured him. "The lab techs have informed me that they need an additional fifteen minutes to launch the DRSV."

"DRSV?" Wyman asked.

"Deep Reconnaissance Submersible Vehicle," Trudeau replied. He pointed over his shoulder to the main sub hanging over the submersion pool. "It seats six," he continued, "with enough room for…" he let his sentence trail off as he spotted the two Tereshkova crewman behind the Vice President. "Sir, if I may ask, what are they doing here?"

"I've beefed up my security force," the Vice President answered. "These men already had the screening and clearance, so they were the obvious choice. You remember Captain Alexander Hull, Captain Jennifer Hull, and Ensign Jensen?"

Trudeau nodded. "Sir, I don't want to seem out of line, but were they the best choices? I have several well-trained soldiers at my command who would have been much better choices."

"I've made my decision, Commander," Wyman said, over enunciating the man's rank, "that should be enough for you. Let's get on with this."

Trudeau nodded quickly after the reprimand. Hitting several buttons on his wrist computer, he tapped in the station's frequency. "Wet Lab Control, this is Trudeau, do you copy?"

"This is Control," came the response over his comm, a slight hint of static in the frequency. "We have you, Commander. Go ahead."

Hull leaned close to Jansen. "Why is there static?" he asked in a hushed voice. "It should be clear as a bell inside the station."

Jansen nodded. "Checking."

Hull leaned over to Jennifer. "Why don't you head up to Control? See if there's a problem up there."

Jennifer patted Hull on the shoulder. "I'm on it." Turning, she was quickly out of the door.

"Control, we are ready to begin prelaunch countdown on the main DRSV. Confirm?"

"Confirmed, Commander. Commencing countdown. Have your men ready to board in five minutes next to the main submersion pool."

"Acknowledged, Control." Leaving the comm channel open, he turned to the Vice President. "If you'll excuse me, sir."

Wyman nodded.

Trudeau turned and walked toward his men, once again barking orders. The black-clad soldiers began to move all their necessary equipment toward the main pool.

Wyman turned back and looked at Hull. "Anything?" Hull turned to Jansen.

"There seems to be an abnormally high concentration of radiation in the Wet Lab," Jansen replied. "Can't get a solid fix on it though."

"Could it be left over from the last mission three weeks ago?" Wyman wondered.

"I'm not sure, Mr. Vice President," Jansen answered. "It could be, or it could be Jupiter. Maybe there's a crack in the ice and some of the planet's radiation seeped down into the water."

"Are we in any immediate danger?" Hull asked.

Jansen checked his tracer again and shook his head. "I wouldn't want to stay in here more than an hour," he breathed. "But right now, we're fine."

"Where will you be observing the mission from, Mr. Vice President?" Hull asked.

"I'll be up in Wet Lab Control," Wyman answered. "They'll have a direct feed from the men's EV suits and the DRSV, and we'll be able to talk with Commander Trudeau if the need arises."

As the soldiers moved toward the DRSV, the fourth soldier reached down and typed a single command into his wrist computer: EXECUTE.

The standard blue background of his computer screen was replaced with red as an ominous thermal gauge appeared. Near the top, a blank line was marked across the gauge, indicating the temperature required to activate his modifications. As the pack on his back began to heat up, he could feel the warmth radiating into his suit. It was only a matter of seconds before the suit's warning systems would go into effect. Watching the temperature raise on the display inside his helmet, he saw steam begin to collect on the transparasteel visor. As the suit hit the critical mark, he smiled. The suit's sensors didn't trigger the alarms. His modifications to the computer coil had worked.

Jansen's tracer began to beep incessantly. Tapping several buttons on the bottom, he killed the alarm and watched several warnings appear. "Captain…"

Hull turned to look at Jansen.

"I've got a major thermal build-up occurring in the lab," he said, rechecking his readings.

"Where is it?" Ansil asked urgently.

Jansen swept his tracer across the lab, stopping on Trudeau's men. "It's right there," he said, pointing to the soldiers. "I can't be more specific due to the radiation in here."

Gordon and Ansil drew their pulse pistols and started toward the soldiers. Hull keyed his wristcomm, "Commander Trudeau, we have a problem." The fourth soldier heard the signal in his helmet. Gritting his teeth, he snapped the restraining strap off his holster and held his hand on the grip of his pulse pistol.

"What is it?" Trudeau asked quickly, not in the mood to be playing games with the spacer.

"We've got a major thermal build-up in your area," Hull said quickly. "Hold your position."

Trudeau lifted his hand as he stopped. His men followed suit. "This better be good," he muttered under his breath.

Gordon and Ansil charged across the Wet Lab, stopping just shy of the soldiers. With their weapons still drawn, each activated their wristcomms. "This is definitely the source of the thermal signature," Ansil reported from across the lab. Walking in, the two security guards stayed on their toes.

The fourth soldier wrapped his fingers carefully around the grip of his weapon, but kept it holstered.

Gordon moved closer to the soldiers. "Please hold your positions," he said as his eyes worked over each soldier. "This is official Earth Gov business. Failure to comply will result in the use of deadly force," he warned them ominously. "Stand your ground," he said again as a bead of sweat rolled down his face. Heat seemed to be radiating off the four soldiers. As he moved further to his left, the temperature grew. He nodded to Ansil.

"All right, buddy," Ansil said bravely, "What the hell is going on?" He reached in and slapped his open palm on the fourth soldier's EV suit. With a shriek of pain, he immediately pulled his seared hand back.

As Gordon's attention was turned to his comrade, the fourth soldier drew his pulse pistol and squeezed off a single shot into the elder guard's midsection.

As the man fell to the ground, the fourth soldier threw a vicious elbow into the helmet of the next soldier. Taking a step back, he grabbed Ansil and twisted him around. Pressing him to his suit, he wrapped his arm across Ansil's suit. "Anyone moves and he dies," the soldier warned. The smell of burning cloth and flesh began to waft in the air as Ansil screamed in pain.

Hull and Jansen moved in front of the Vice President. Jansen held his tracer up for his captain and the Vice President to clearly see the reading.

"Jesus Christ," Wyman muttered under his breath.

"What the hell do you think you're doing, solder?" Hull asked quickly. "You have enough thermal explosives strapped to your body to put a major hole in this station. You have to realize, if that bomb goes off in this room, there's an entire alien ocean just dying to get in here."

"That's the plan," the soldier replied ghoulishly. "None of you will have the artifact. It belongs to the civilization of this moon, not to you!"

"Damned insurgents," Wyman cursed.

"Will a pulse shot set off the explosives?" Hull asked Jansen over his shoulder.

"Hard to say," Jansen replied, "but either way, he's building up to detonation really quickly. We better do some—"

The high-pitched sound of a pulse pistol being discharged cut through the Wet Lab like a knife.

Hull spun to see the soldier drop Ansil's dead body and stumble back toward the main pool with a smoking hole in the front of his suit. Twisting his head around, he saw Trudeau holding the weapon. Hull leapt off the balls of his feet and hit a dead sprint toward the pool. "Don't let that man fall in!"

Two of the remaining three soldiers spun and grabbed for the soldier, but they were too late. Falling backwards, the insurgent hit the edge of the submersion pool and fell awkwardly inside with a splash. Hull skidded to a stop and placed his hands on the edge. He watched the black EV suit sink lifelessly down toward the bottom.

Hull started to dive in after him, but the three remaining soldiers quickly grabbed and restrained him. "You can't go in there, Captain," they yelled. "If the temperature of the water doesn't kill you, the pressure will."

Hull broke free of the men's grasp. He looked helplessly down at the man lying on the bottom. He quickly turned to Jansen. "Is the build-up still taking place?"

Jansen took another reading and nodded. "The temperature of the water slowed it slightly, but it's still building up."

"How long?"

Jansen hit another button on his tracer. "I really think we need to get the hell out of here."

"We can't just leave," Hull yelled. "The explosion will take out the entire Wet Lab!"

The Vice President grabbed Hull's shoulder. "We don't have a choice, Captain. Move!"

Hull complied reluctantly. Turning, he patted Jansen on the back and charged for the door. He keyed his wristcomm, "Control, this is Captain Hull."

"This is Control. Alex, it's Jennifer. What the hell is going on down there?"

"No time for an explanation, Jennifer," Hull breathed as he continued to charge for the door. "Raise all emergency shields and lock down the Wet Lab as soon as the Vice President's party is through the doors. Prepare for an explosion and decompression. Wait for my next signal."

"Acknowledged," Jennifer responded.

Yanking open the pressure door, they felt a rumble below the station. The floor around them instantly buckled up and three quarters of the far wall was shredded in a plume of fire and water. Water surged like a geyser into the Wet Lab through the newly created holes. Pushing the Vice President through the door, Hull grabbed Jansen and charged inside. Holding onto the locking mechanism with all his strength, Hull tried to keep the door open for Trudeau and his men. He watched as one of the soldiers was lifted by the column of water and smashed against the nearest wall. His helmet was crushed in like an empty can.

"Close the door!"

Hull wasn't sure he heard the message through his wristcomm correctly. He hesitated.

"Close the damned door now, Captain Hull!"

Understanding Trudeau's message the second time, he tried to regain his footing amidst the rushing water. Jansen pulled himself up and grabbed the latch with Hull. The two pushed with all their might against the water. Hull turned his head to see a control panel on the wall near the door. Kicking it with his booted foot, he heard the door's powerful hydraulic motors begin to whine as they forced the door shut. Once closed, Jansen quickly spun the locking mechanism, sealing the door.

"Control," Hull yelled into his wristcomm, "shields!"

Through the small porthole on the door, he saw the golden flicker of the shields being activated in the dark water. He searched for any sign of Trudeau and his men, but could see nothing. Turning, he lifted the Vice President out of the bone chilling, knee-deep water. "Are you okay, sir?"

Wyman nodded. "I can't seem to get warm, Captain."

Hull nodded and turned to Jansen. "Get the Vice President out of here, Ensign. Take him up to control."

Jansen nodded. "You got it, Skipper."

Hull cringed again at the name, but this wasn't the time or place to discipline the young officer. Turning back, Hull waded through the freezing water and stood in front of the door. Peering into the water, he keyed his wristcomm, “Commander Trudeau, do you read me?” He waited for a response.

“Commander Trudeau, this is Captain Hull. Do you copy?” Silence. “Jennifer, this is Hull. Do you see Commander Trudeau and his men?”

“That’s a negative, Alex. I couldn’t make my hand out in front of my face in that murky water.”

Hull ran his hand over his mouth. Turning away, he started to slog through the water. Stopping, he glanced back over his shoulder one more time at the door. He heard the sharp sizzle of static on his wristcomm. He quickly lifted it and placed his fingers on the frequency buttons. “Commander Trudeau, do you copy? Commander Trudeau—”

“This is Trudeau,” he responded through the static. “My transmitter took quite a beating, but I’m okay. Two of my men survived the blast as well. We were able to activate our new shields in time to save our asses.”

Hull smiled with relief. “Are you going to be okay in there for a while?”

“Affirmative,” Trudeau answered. “O2 levels are good.”

“We’ll get back to you as soon as we know anything, Commander. Hull out.” Snapping his wristcomm into standby mode, he headed up the hall to join Jansen and the Vice President.

CHAPTER TEN

The destruction of the Wet Lab was total. What the explosion didn't claim, the rushing water had. Looking out through the Control windows, they stared at the gaping hole in the bottom of Europa Station. It had taken hours for the silt in the water to settle enough so they could actually make a visual inspection. The explosion had torn out nearly the entire floor, south and north walls, and portions of the adjoining facilities. Structural scans of the pod showed three of its fifty-five support beams had been broken, while another five showed visible signs of stress. The pod wasn't in any immediate danger of collapsing to the ocean floor, but the center where the Wet Lab had been was starting to sag slightly. All the equipment and two DRSVs sat at the bottom of the Europan ocean. It was a major setback for the project.

"Goddamned insurgents," the Vice President roared as he paced the floor of the Control room. "It's not enough for them to bring down an entire Triumph class ship anymore. Now they have to destroy a multi-billion-dollar installation on another planet."

"Moon," TC corrected. "Europa is not an actual planet, although it is certainly almost as big as the planet Mercury and easily larger than the binary planet of Pluto. It's correct classification is a satellite of—"

"Will someone shut him up?" the Vice President growled.

Hull quickly held his finger up to his lips. TC nodded knowingly. The big bot was just trying to be helpful.

"They call themselves the Voxx," Wyman laughed at the preposterous name. "They claim they're trying to purify the human race. The only thing those Goddamned bastards want to purify is their frakkin' water. If they would spend half the resources they do on diplomatic means instead of making bombs, they would probably convince us all to mothball the fleet. But no, they have to go around blowing things up."

The Vice President had been on this particular rant, an extension of his earlier one that had lasted almost an hour, for at least forty minutes now. He showed no signs of stopping either. As the technicians worked to secure the station, he had continued to pace the floor and spit venom. Hull's entire crew, including Jennifer and TC-10, had gathered in the station to provide security for Wyman in the absence of Gordon and Ansil. The captain's thought had been safety in numbers, but the earlier incident that left four people dead and destroyed a good portion of pod one spoke contrary to that theory. In either case, it felt better to have the entire crew here, rather than scattered across the station.

With Ramirez still roaming free, Hull didn't feel safe. He and the Vice President had spoken earlier in the day about arresting Ramirez. Their evidence was concrete enough, but they didn't know how the security force here would take that. They might be loyal to Ramirez and turn on the Vice President, or they could willingly haul him off to the stockade. It all boiled down to what kind of boss Ramirez has been to these men, and from what Hull had seen, he had tried to become everyone's best friend. They were in a sticky situation.

"The mission has to move forward," the Vice President said, ending his current rant. It was the same conclusion he had come to almost an hour ago. They weren't sure if he was speaking about the artifact recovery mission, or the mission to explore space in general. He had never been exceptionally clear on that point, and none of them wanted to incur another rant, so they hadn't asked. "We have to acquire the artifact."

Cody sat forward in shock. She had to say something. "With all due respect, Mr. Vice President, are you out of your mind? Do you seriously expect anyone to go out there and get that," Cody paused, searching for the words, "whatever the hell it is for you after what we've just seen?"

"This incident, if anything," Jennifer added from across the control room, "should lock down the station for quite some time. No one will be able to get in or out of the water until all the structural inspections and repairs are completed."

"You're both forgetting one very important point," the Vice President said quickly, "the station chief is a friggin' insurgent! Unless we all want to stay here for the next year or so while repairs are completed, we're not going to be able to monitor everyone that gets in the water!"

"The Vice is right," Chris nodded. "With Ramirez in the big chair, it's only a matter of time before the insurgents claim control of the artifact. We need to utilize the Vice President's power while we're here."

"I agree," Jansen said.

"I tend to side with Lieutenant Cody on this one," Kira spoke softly. She had been quiet ever since arriving on the scene and witnessing the devastation first-hand. "I can't see the sense in sending more people to their deaths over what could be nothing more than a rock formation." She swung her feet off the console and sat up in her chair. "If the rock is that important to the insurgents, let them have it. No one listened to them before, no one will after they have it. They will continue to blow things up and eventually, everyone will forget about the artifact."

The Vice President slowly turned to Hull. He had been standing silently in the corner of the room staring out into the vast pit of destruction that had previously been the Wet Lab ever since this conversation had started. "Captain Hull," the Vice President said sternly, "I would like to know what you think."

Hull slowly turned and scanned over the faces of his crew, his friends. Turning toward the Vice President, he took a long breath. "Three good men died here today, but it could have been a lot worse. These insurgents are making us fearful of living in our own solar system. We can't stop at a station to refuel without the threat of one of them slipping a bomb into our engines, or travel through open space without the constant threat of their pirate attacks. Hell, I break into a damned cold sweat every time I fire up the engines on the Tereshkova. This is not the environment I want to live in. I will not give them one more thing to fuel their cause, not one more thing. Mr. Vice President, you asked what I think about the situation?"

The Vice President nodded.

Hull stepped forward and snapped to attention. "I volunteer to go on the mission to retrieve the artifact."

Hull's crew stared at him in disbelief.

Wyman nodded with a smile. He knew he liked this man for a reason. "Any other volunteers?"

Jansen stood. "Count me in, sir." Hull nodded to his science officer.

"You can count me in, Skipper," Chris said with a nod and wink.

"I would also like to accompany you, Captain," TC said quickly, "but as the pressure of the water would easily crush my frame and render me a useless hunk of junk, I'm going to have to sit this one out."

Hull laughed out loud. "Thanks, TC. We need you on the ship anyway."

"Thank goodness," TC said with relief, "I thought you were going to make me go anyway."

"I'm in," Jennifer said after a moment, "if you'll have me."

The Vice President's smile broadened. "Two captains are better than one." Cody looked at the rest of her teammates and immediately felt guilty. They were showing such courage in the face of danger. She would not let her captain down. "You're going to need navigation on this mission," she said, standing up. "I'm in."

"You're also going to need a tactical officer on this little excursion of yours," Kira said as she stood up. "I'm in, but only to protect your butt, Captain."

"I appreciate the gesture," Hull smiled. He turned to the Vice President. "I have my team. When do we launch?"

"I need to get with Chief Ramirez," Wyman spat the name. "I know there are auxiliary DRSVs on the station and alternate Wet Labs. I just need to get 'official' permission to use them. You'll also need to retrieve the alternate EV suits from the Tereshkova to use on the dive. They were specially equipped for this mission." The Vice President checked his watch. "It's just past noon now. We'll meet down here at sixteen hundred hours. I don't expect my meeting with Ramirez to last more than ten or fifteen minutes. I don't want to give those bastards any time to set up another booby trap. We need to get moving on this one as soon as possible. Agreed?"

"What about Commander Trudeau?" Hull asked.

"He won't be ready for another mission by that time. They pulled him back inside almost an hour ago. He and his two men caught in the explosion suffered internal injuries. They're down for the count on this one," he said gravely. "I'll go check on him after my meeting with Ramirez."

"Good. While you're on that, I want Chris, TC and Katrina to retrieve the spare EV suits from the Tereshkova," Hull ordered. "Jansen, you and Kira are in charge of sweeping the new Wet Lab. I want nothing left to chance this time. Captain Hull," he said, looking at Jennifer, "you and I need to study."

"What exactly does that mean?" Jennifer asked.

"If the Vice President will permit us, I would like to learn everything we can about the artifact we're going out to retrieve. We need to look at maps of the area, research data, everything you have."

Wyman nodded. "The information will be at your disposal, Captains. I'll provide you with my security key for the files. You can access them via your ship or the station's network."

"Thank you, Mr. Vice President." Hull turned and looked at his crew. "Does everyone understand their orders?" Hull waited for each to nod. He looked at each member individually. "You're doing a good thing today." He beamed with pride. "End of speech. Let's get to work."

It had awakened.

***

Buried deep within the mud and silt of the ocean's bottom, it began to reverberate to life. Its automatic defenses, left intact by the creators, began to shut down. There was no more use for them. Sensors indicated some kind of abrupt seismic event had triggered the start mechanism. Running through various diagnostic programs, it checked to make sure its systems were undamaged. It encountered several errors while accessing components related to internal memory. It tried to repair the corrupted files but found they had been irrevocably lost. It tried again to salvage the information and move it to a new file to no avail. As a last resort, it cycled through its memory to the last given instructions. Accessing the file, it stored it in a secondary backup and began to implement the instructions. Key pieces of data seemed to be missing, but they were determined irrelevant to completing the instructions. They, at least, were complete and very clear.

It's diagnostic programs continued on beyond their programming and data files. Switching to hardware, it came to the abrupt realization that nearly sixty percent of it had been damaged or lost completely. Confused, it tried to access its chronometer to understand how long it had been dormant. As the numbers rolled since the last time it had been activated, its confusion swelled. Nearly four billion cycles had passed. That was far too long. That bordered on catastrophic. Trying to access its network, it failed to connect with any of the others. Activating its scanners, it scanned the moon for any signs of its creators, but found nothing that matched their chemical makeup or unique genetic signature—although it did find a species currently residing on the planet who came close. It quickly ruled them out as its creators and turned off its sensors. It was alone and severely damaged. It would not be able to execute its instructions in this state. It had to institute repairs first.

It quickly began reassigning sectors within itself to supervise the repairs. Systems essential to completing the instructions would be repaired first, leaving secondary systems offline. It would finish its creator's task, even if they were no longer here to witness it.

CHAPTER ELEVEN

Jansen and Kira were their first to make it to their assignments. Stepping through the pressure doors into Wet Lab Two, they glanced around the room. It wasn't quite as big as Wet Lab One, but it had everything necessary to complete the mission at hand. In the center of the room was the huge submersion pool with a single DRSV hanging above it. This pool was roughly half the size of Wet Lab One's, and designed to accommodate the size of the DRSV and little more. The water in the pool looked calm and serene in stark contrast to the ocean they had been watching devour Wet Lab One. This lab was located on almost the opposite side of the station in pod fifteen and it seemed it hadn't been used in a while. The massive control room windows were completely dark and showed no signs of activity, even though Kira had requested two techs meet them here.

Jansen reached into his uniform pocket and produced a second, smaller tracer. "This one's not quite as powerful as the one I'm using," he said apologetically, "but it should still serve our purpose."

Kira accepted the small, black, rectangular tracer and thumbed the power switch at the bottom. It only took a matter of seconds for the device to power up and beep once to signal its readiness. "How did you come into possession of two illegal tracers?"

Jansen smiled, unwilling to reveal his sources. "I have my ways." He tapped the screen on his tracer several times and began his scan.

"Why don't we just use regular scanner pads?" Kira asked, feeling a little nervous about using illegal equipment. "They would suit our purposes fine."

"Probably," Jansen agreed, "but I've outfitted these two babies with some special modifications not exactly allowed by EGCC regulations. The Earth Gov Communication Council doesn't allow any device to lock on, interrupt, or hijack communication signals," Jansen said with a smirk, "mine can. I also have upgraded scanning and interface software that can crack any electronic device known to man. The government tends to frown on that as well."

"I can't believe our little twenty-year-old science officer is a slicer," Kira said with a laugh. Activating her tracer, she began to scan the area. "It just boggles the mind."

"Why?" Jansen asked curiously.

"It just seems your career would be more important to you than a few illegal toys. You could seriously get booted out of the UESA for just having these."

"The captain doesn't seem to mind."

Kira shook her head. "It isn't him you have to worry about. It's some other jealous snitch that sees you with these."

"Are you trying to tell me something?"

Kira smiled and laughed. "I own you now, Ensign."

"You're blackmailing me?" Jansen turned and looked at his superior officer in shock.

"I don't like that word," Kira said, sweeping her tracer across the pool, "it sounds so nefarious. I prefer the term 'extortion'. Sounds more," she paused and smiled deviously, “evil.” The word sounded even worse filtered through her Russian accent.

“What are you going to do?” Jansen asked nervously.

“I’m thinking,” she paused, playing up the moment, “you will take all my KP for the next month.”

“Kitchen duty?” Jansen shook his head, “I’d rather be kicked out of the UESA.”

Kira laughed out loud. Reaching over, she slapped Jansen on the back, “I’m just kidding, nugget. I wouldn’t do that to you. You need to loosen up a little bit.”

“You are an evil woman,” Jansen said with a breath. “I like that about you.” Kira winked at the junior officer. “You take that side of the Wet Lab, I’ll start working on this side.”

Jansen nodded. “Sounds like a plan, Commander.”

“Let’s get this done quickly,” Kira said as she started to walk away. “After seeing the other Wet Lab, this place gives me the creeps.”

Jansen nodded to Kira. “I couldn’t agree more.”

***

“This is astounding,” Jennifer said, staring at the screen. “If this is what all the big wigs think it is, this could be the most ground-breaking discovery in the history of mankind.” She traced her finger over the artifact on the screen, transfixed by it.

They were sitting in the living room of the Vice President’s quarters. Jennifer was seated on the floor with several pads scattered around her while

Hull was perched on the edge of the couch staring at papers stacked on the coffee table. The door was locked, and security measures had been activated. They didn't want anyone to know, or see what they were looking at. They had even gone so far as to cover the cameras in the room with a towel, or a sheet of paper taped over the lenses.

Hull nodded as he looked over geological maps or Europa's surface. "I can't believe how incomplete these are. Only a fraction of the surface has been mapped."

"Aren't you concerned about the artifact?"

Hull nodded. "Yes, but I'm more concerned about the mission. I want to know what we're heading in to."

Jennifer turned her attention away from the pad she held and looked over Hull's shoulder at the maps. "Do you even know how to read those?" Hull sighed. "Sort of."

"Here," she said, flipping the map over so it faced the correct direction, "let me take a look." She began to quickly study the topographical image before her. "It looks like there's an underwater mountain range here," she said, pointing to the left side of the map, "and the station is only a few kilometers from a deep trench. What are the coordinates for the artifact?"

"That's part of the problem," Hull said. "We don't know. All we have to go on is the last reported coordinates of the research team before they headed back to the station. They never made a proper report."

"Probably because they went nuts as soon as they returned," Jennifer speculated. "What are their last known coordinates?"

Hull checked his pad, then traced his finger over the map. "Due north of the station about twenty-five kilometers."

"It could be anywhere along this trench," she tapped on the map. "I wish we had exact coordinates."

Hull nodded. "That would make our job easier."

"Alex," Jennifer said slowly, sitting back, "how do we know we won't go crazy looking at that thing?" She lifted one of the pads next to her. "It says in the chief medical officer's report that one of the research team actually tried to scratch his own eyes out."

Hull turned his attention back to Jennifer, looking her squarely in the eyes. "I can't make any promises." He took a long, deep breath. "But I do know this could be a one-way trip."

"What are you saying?"

"It's a possibility we all have to face," Hull said sternly. "We may not be coming back."

Jennifer fell silent.

"You don't have to go." She nodded. "I know."

"You're getting married soon. You might want to think about your future." She looked up at her ex-husband calmly. "But I can't look to the future at the expense of the present." She bit her lip for a moment. "Let's say for a moment that the insurgents beat us to the artifact and recover it for themselves. What then?"

"Probably renewed focus on their cause," Hull speculated. "If you had something that proved all your points, wouldn't that strengthen your resolve?"

"Undoubtedly," she said. "If they get this thing, a lot of innocent people are going to die, aren't they?"

Hull leaned back on the couch, but never broke eye contact with Jennifer. "That would be my guess."

Both fell silent for a moment as they considered the ramifications of the events unfolding around them. They were no longer innocent spectators; they now held the destiny of mankind in their hands.

"We can't let them have it," Jennifer said quickly. "I still want to go on this mission."

Hull smiled. "Good to have you along, Captain."

"This isn't some kind of ploy," Jennifer asked with a slightly bemused grin on her face, "is it?"

He cocked his head slightly. "What are you talking about?"

"This isn't some hair-brained scheme of yours to make me fall in love with you again, is it?" Jennifer leaned on the coffee table. "Acting all heroic and such?"

Hull laughed. "I hadn't thought about that. Is it working?"

Jennifer quickly turned away and snatched a pad off the floor. "Absolutely not."

Hull shrugged. "We should get back to work. We still have a lot of data to go through."

She nodded, unwilling to look directly into his eyes. As he went back to his maps, she stared up from her pad at his face. She couldn't help wondering if she were making a huge mistake. Was this new man in her life the one she truly loved, or just a pale substitute of a former relationship? Pulling her hair away from her face, she went back to work. She had to wait until the events of today played out before she could make up her mind. The stress of the moment couldn't be allowed to influence her decision. She had to look at everything with a clear mind. Although, she thought with a soft smile, last night was wonderful.

***

Three of the station's security force had been assigned to the Vice President in the absence of his bodyguards. None of whom had any military training, but were instead volunteers culled from the ranks of the UESA. The three men, dressed in black jumpsuits with a yellow band around the upper sleeve of each arm, buzzed nervously around the Vice President, their hands on their holsters strapped to their hips. Wyman shook his head as he headed across the promenade deck. His new security "force" was drawing more attention to him than having a dozen red, blinking balloons tied to his head while shooting a pistol randomly in the air. It didn't matter though, thankfully. After the explosion in Wet Lab One, the entire station had been locked down. Every shop, every restaurant, every business on the promenade was locked down and closed up. Not a single soul could be seen anywhere on the massive deck.

Arriving at the side of the promenade deck, Wyman entered the administration portion of the station through double automatic doors. Walking down the long corridor, he spotted the lavish entrance at the end. It was designed with translucent windows in them with Chief Ramirez's name laser-etched in thick, black letters. Wyman was dreading this moment. He knew Ramirez was in bed with the enemy, but he couldn't act on that information just yet. There was still work that needed to be done, and alerting the insurgents their main operative had been found out and arrested would surely bring them screaming down on the station like a flock of vultures. This petty man meant little to him, but the organization he was tied to did.

Wyman stopped and looked at the door. He waited patiently, but his patience was quickly dwindling. "Well?"

His three security men looked to the Vice President and then to each other. The procedure was obviously lost on them.

"Go in the damned door first," Wyman said angrily, "to check for possible security risks on the other side."

The first security man quickly apologized to the Vice President, drew his pulse pistol and charged through the door. Looking around the station chief's waiting room, the security officer nodded once at the personal assistant seated behind the only desk. Opening the main doors again, he turned to the Vice President. "All clear, sir."

"Jesus," Wyman muttered, shaking his head. Walking in the room, the Vice President pointed at Ramirez's assistant. "I need to see the Chief right now," he paused, "make it happen."

"I'm sorry, sir, Mr. Ramirez is in a very important meeting right now," the assistant replied as politely as possible. "If you'd like to take a seat, I'd be happy to schedule an appointment for you."

Wyman shook his head. "I said make it happen. If you don't, I will."

"Threatening will get you nowhere, sir," the assistant began. "If you will just take a seat, I will schedule an—"

"Do you know who I am?" Wyman asked.

"Yes, Mr. Vice President," the assistant nodded, "I know who you are. That, however, won't get you into that office any faster."

"Crack it," the Vice President said, pointing to Ramirez's door. Without hesitation, one of the security guards moved to the door and activated the console. Keying in the override code, the system chimed in response. The red light on the console snapped to green as the door automatically slid open.

"You can't do that, sir," the assistant protested.

As two of the security guards moved into Ramirez's office, the Vice President leaned over on the assistant's desk and motioned for him to come near. "Son," Wyman said with a smirk, "if I were you, I would start looking for a new job."

The stunned assistant could say nothing in retaliation.

Moving into Ramirez's office with the final security guard in tow, the Vice President stood in front of the chief's desk. Ramirez, currently in a videoconference, glanced up to see the Vice President standing over his desk. Without any significant reaction, he turned back to his monitor.

"I'm sorry, gentlemen, I'm going to have to wrap this call up," he said pleasantly. "My next appointment is a little early. Thank you, and we'll be in touch." Reaching over, he killed the feed and ended the call. Spinning slowly in his chair, he looked calmly at Wyman. "What can I do for you?"

Wyman wanted to reach across the desk and pull the traitor up by his scrawny neck. Taking a deep breath in through his nose, he slowly exhaled it through his mouth. He had to be civil a while longer. At least long enough to obtain the artifact. "After this morning's incident," Wyman began slowly, "there has been a change in plans."

"Understandably," Ramirez agreed confidently. He was letting a bit of his true colors show. "I assume the mission has been scrapped until the safety of the station can be ensured and repairs can be made?"

"Actually," Wyman paused, taking great pleasure in the moment, "the mission is moving forward."

"What?" Ramirez leapt up from his seat and slammed his fists to his desk. "After the loss of life and severe damage to the station, how can you even contemplate going ahead with this mission?"

"The loss of life is regrettable," Wyman nodded, "but it only proved one thing to me: the insurgents are blood-thirsty cowards who are willing to stop at nothing to attain their goals." He watched Ramirez's face twitch slightly as he spoke. "It has become clear that we must move ahead and recover the artifact."

Ramirez started to protest, but Wyman waved him off.

"A new mission team has already been selected," Wyman informed him. "I am merely here to let you know another attempt is going to be made."

"Where will you launch from?" Ramirez asked finally. "What transportation will you use? When is the mission scheduled to take place?"

"I'm sorry," Wyman said with a smirk. "That information has become classified." He turned and started out of the office.

"You can't cut me out of the loop, I'm the Goddamned Station Chief," Ramirez yelled.

Wyman could hear the panic in Ramirez's voice and it brought a smile to his face. Motioning to his security guards, they moved quickly out of the administrative wing of the facility. Once back out on the promenade deck, Wyman lifted his arm and keyed his wristcomm. "Captain?"

"Yes, Mr. Vice President?" Hull's voice answered. "Is all nearing readiness?"

"We're just about there. This mission will launch on time."

"Good," Wyman laughed, "because I think I just put a major burr up the chief's ass."

"Acknowledged," Hull said with a laugh.

Snapping off his wristcomm, Wyman turned to his security guards. "Take me to the main infirmary. I want to speak with Commander Trudeau."

***

"Come on, TC," Chris shouted from the airlock, "get those crates over here!"

TC pushed the hoverdolly through the main doors that led into the airlock.

Using a dolly to move objects in zero gravity was harder than it sounded. Objects that weren't secured to it had a tendency to just float off. Everything had to be strapped down. "Why don't you haul your bag of bones over here and help?" the big bot squawked.

"I don't know what you're complaining about," Chris laughed. "It's not like those crates weigh anything right now. Plus, you're a big, strapping robot. It can't be that difficult."

"You two argue like an old married couple," Cody speculated. "Can we hurry this up? We're on a deadline."

"Better listen to the lady, TC," Chris prodded. "Get a move on."

TC maneuvered the dolly toward the main airlock and stopped. "Bite me, old man." Reaching out, he activated the lock. Stepping out of the way, he motioned to the dolly. "It's all yours."

Chris floated around to the back of the dolly and placed both hands on the bar. Lowering his feet, he anchored them against the floor and prepared to push the dolly ahead.

As the door slid open revealing the cylindrical halls of Europa Prime, the three stopped dead in their tracks. Standing in the way wearing magnetic boots, were four of the station's security personnel. Three had pulse pistols aimed at the Tereshkova's crew, while the other held a pulse rifle at the ready.

"What the hell is this?" Cody asked angrily.

"This vessel is to be searched for contraband," the first security guard stated. "All transfers of personnel and cargo must be immediately suspended until the search is complete."

"On whose orders?" Cody yelled.

"By order of Chief Ramirez," the guard answered. "If you do not step aside and cooperate with the investigation, you will be forcefully restrained." All four security guards took a step forward. One of the guards looked back at the hulking form of TC-10. "Please shut down your bot for the duration of this investigation."

"I won't," Chris protested.

The security guards had no time for this.

"Look at him," the engineer pointed to his friend, "he's not exactly the newest design in the fleet. If we shut him down, we may never be able to reboot him."

TC's nervousness jumped up by a factor of ten.

Chris pressed his point. "If I can't reboot our bot, who is going to replace him?"

"If we find illegal contraband on this ship," the first security guard said, pointing his weapon at Chris' head, "it won't really matter if your robot doesn't work anymore. You'll all be arrested and your ship seized. Deactivate the robot," the security guard growled, "now!"

Chris looked to Cody and then to TC. Gritting his teeth, he shrugged. Turning, he floated back to the big bot. "Sorry, pal," he whispered. "I won't let you die," Chris added, "I promise."

Opening a panel on TC's chest, he quickly keyed in the security code that gave him access to the bot's programming. Chris instituted an immediate shutdown. The bot took a step back and clamped himself to the wall. His red eye scanned over the security guards, then settled on Chris. With one shudder, he shut down. His glowing red eye faded and his head fell limply forward.

The security guards moved into the airlock and closed the door. As the three with pulse pistols disappeared into the ship, the fourth rounded Chris and Cody into the corner next to TC's deactivated body. Leaning back against the wall, the guard kept his rifle leveled at the two. Cody slid behind Chris and turned away from the guard. Reaching down carefully, she keyed her wristcomm.

"Captain," she whispered, looking back at the guards.

"Go ahead, Lieutenant," Hull responded. "We have a problem."

CHAPTER TWELVE

With his three security guards standing around him, the Vice President stared through the large window into the medical bay. Trudeau and his two remaining men lay quietly on raised beds as a collection of monitors above each checked their vital statistics. The room was dark except for the glare of the screens and a small light bank just above the beds. A single nurse moved about the room attending them. From behind, Quentin moved up and joined the Vice President as he looked through the window at his men.

“Helluva thing,” Quentin said slowly. “Couldn’t believe it when I heard it.” Wyman pulled himself away from the window and addressed the doctor.

“Dr. Kelly,” he greeted the doctor, remembering his name.

“Mr. Vice President,” Quentin returned the greeting. “This was the first insurgent attack on Europa Station.”

Wyman nodded. “Bastards.” He tried to reel in his anger. “What are their conditions?”

“The two lieutenants,” Quentin glanced down at his pad, “Rockwell and Macintyre fared a little better than Commander Trudeau did. From the account I heard, they already had their EV suits on when the explosion occurred. That fact alone probably saved their lives.” He looked at his pad again, glancing over their individual charts. “Each had a few broken bones, and Lieutenant Macintyre had a very minor concussion, but those were relatively easy to repair. They’re just resting now.

They should be discharged by tomorrow. We're keeping them here for observation."

"And Commander Trudeau?"

"His case was a little more severe," Quentin admitted. "He's slipped into a coma. When he came in, he was suffering from severe hypothermia. We almost had to amputate his right arm, but we found a way to save it. Apparently," Quentin said, paging to his chart, "he didn't have his helmet on when the blast took place. He took in a lot of that freezing water before he got his helmet locked on. It stayed in his suit, weighing him down, and unfortunately, almost freezing him to death."

"Damn," Wyman breathed.

It could have been worse," Quentin tried to comfort the Vice President. "He was lucky he didn't drown."

"How long will he be in the coma?"

"Hard to say," Quentin answered. "It could be a week, a day, an hour, or for the rest of his life. He suffered some pretty dramatic damage to his brain. We have no way of knowing for sure."

The Vice President patted Quentin on the shoulder. "Thank you, Dr. Kelly." Quentin nodded. "Sir," he said slowly, "if I may ask?"

Wyman nodded.

Quentin gritted his teeth. "Have you caught the bastards responsible for this yet?"

"We're very close, Doctor," Wyman said quietly. "We have to complete our mission first, then we're gonna bring the whole lot of traitors here to justice. I promise I won't let this attack go unpunished."

Quentin extended his hand. "Thank you, Mr. Vice President." Wyman shook the doctor's hand with a smile. "Thank you, Doctor."

"Mr. Vice President," Quentin said slowly, "there's something you need to see." He slowly reached into his pocket and produced the datapad with the information he had saved earlier. He handed it to Wyman. "There was nothing wrong with any of the men who came in contact with the artifact. They were all completely healthy. This information proves it."

Wyman looked at the doctor curiously. "Then what killed them?" Quentin furrowed his brow. "Ramirez."

"How did you get this?" Wyman asked accepting the pad.

"I downloaded it from one of the archaeologist's IC Units just after he died," Quentin admitted.

"Thank you," the Vice President replied and slid the datapad into his pocket.

Quentin turned and walked away, leaving the Vice President alone with his thoughts. As he looked at the three men lying helplessly on their medical beds, he couldn't help but feel responsible. If he had taken more action when Captain Hull had brought the assassination attempt to his attention, this may not have happened. It also reinforced the idea in his mind that the enemy was everywhere. If one could infiltrate Trudeau's specially hand-picked unit… Wyman shook his head. What had more likely happened was the insurgents recruited the soldier based on his psychological profile. Much like the KGB used to do during the Cold War, they turned him to their side with promises of wealth and power. Unsure what they would use him for, it was still better to have a man on the inside, a snake in the garden as it were. Fate had dealt both him and the insurgents this hand, and it had gone down in their favor. Wyman leaned his arm against the glass and balled up his fist. Was the artifact more valuable than a human life? He took a deep breath. That was exactly the decision he was faced with.

His wristcomm chimed. Leaning back from the window, he activated the communicator. "This is Wyman."

"Mr. Vice President," Hull's voice said quickly. "We have a serious problem."

Wyman closed his eyes for a moment. He had been dreading this. "What is it?"

"Chief Ramirez has blocked access to my ship," Hull replied. "He's calling it a contraband inspection."

"That son of a…" he stopped, becoming very aware of where he was. Glancing back over his shoulder, he saw two of the nurses watching him intently from their station. "He can't do that. The Tereshkova is basically a diplomatic vessel. He has no rights there."

"Tell that to my crew being held at gunpoint right now," Hull said. "He's blocked the spare suits from entering the station."

Wyman looked to his security guards, then back to his wristcomm. "Leave this to me. We'll have those suits out of there within the hour."

"That's cutting it awfully close, Mr. Vice President," Hull reminded him. "Don't worry, Captain. I'm about to bring my foot down," Hull said through gritted teeth. "He just pissed off the wrong government official."

***

The door chime buzzed. Standing, Hull turned to Jennifer and pointed to the door. Drawing his pulse pistol, he quietly moved across the floor and stood just inside it. Jennifer pulled her pulse pistol as well and took a few steps away from it. Dropping down to one knee, she aimed carefully at the door and slipped her finger inside the trigger guard. With the lightest pressure, she placed her finger on the trigger. She nodded to Hull. Reaching over, he carefully laid his finger on the control panel and punched in the security code given to him by the Vice President. Accessing the door's view screen, he peered out into the hallway.

With a breath, he holstered his weapon and nodded to Jennifer. Hitting the access button, he opened the door. "Good to see you two."

Jennifer stood to see Kira and Jansen standing just outside the door. Sliding her black pulse pistol back into the holster attached to her right thigh, she relaxed her posture. "How'd the sweep go?"

Kira and Jansen said nothing. A mixture of fear and anger was predominant on their faces. Kira slowly moved her eyes away from the two captains to something just outside Hull's vision.

Hull shook his head. "What the hell is…?"

Jansen motioned with his head in the same direction as Kira.

Hull stared at his two officers. Running his eyes down, he noticed their holsters were empty. Hull's eyes hardened. Snapping his hand down to his holster, he started to draw his pulse pistol when the first black-clad security guard came into view.

Jennifer reacted quickly as well. Reaching out, she grabbed onto Kira's and Jansen's hands. In her peripheral vision, she saw several security guards on both sides of the door. She didn't get a good look, but they seemed ready for war. Ripping Kira and Jansen into the Vice President's quarters, she barely missed a volley of gold plasma projectiles. The door cracked and groaned as the first of the projectiles tore into it. Sparks erupted from the walls just as the three ducked back inside.

Hull started to key in the security code when a blast hit just next to the console and knocked him back. Hitting the floor hard, he tried to catch his breath as he skittered to his feet. "We need to get out of here," he yelled, squeezing off several shots into the doorway.

Kira glanced back over her shoulder. "To where?"

Jennifer drew a bead on a soldier sneaking toward the door. Pressing her shoulder into the wall, she pulled the trigger. The golden burst of energy launched from her weapon and slammed into the guard's chest. As he fell back, two more men took his place firing rapidly into the room. Hitting the floor just inches from her boot, Jennifer tried to throw herself out of the way, but was too slow. The resulting burst of energy blossomed like a mushroom cloud in front of her, searing her suit and hands. Falling back to the floor, she cried out in pain. Kira immediately snatched her weapon and returned fire while Jansen tried to tend Jennifer.

"Jennifer!" Hull shouted. He couldn't get to her as he was pinned down. Hiding behind the small love seat, his position was taking a beating. The couch's right side had already been shredded, and was on fire. He had to think quickly. Looking down at his weapon, a devious grin crossed his face. Snapping open a small panel on the handle of the weapon, he yanked the two wires connecting the power cell free. Crossing the wires, he reattached them to the battery and cranked it up to full power. The weapon began to whine in his hand. "Fire in the hole!"

Tossing the pistol over the couch like a grenade, he turned to see his crewmates moving out of the way. He could see Jansen frantically pulling Jennifer, as Kira provided cover fire. The pistol landed on the floor just in front of the door and skidded out into the hallway. Hull had never done this before, but had read about it in one of the Vice President's mission reports. When he was pinned down at the Battle of Hawaii, he had run out of grenades and had instructed the men to use their weapons. He had eventually won the day. As the makeshift grenade slowed to a stop, the firing stopped as well. They had apparently spotted the weapon.

"Get back!" Hull heard the guards shout.

Taking the opportunity, Hull shot up from his flaming cover, turned and charged toward the kitchen. Diving over the small bar, he hit the cabinets just below the sink, crushing them in. With a moan, he heard the high-pitched whine of the weapon reach its maximum. Rolling onto his knees, he covered his head just as his grenade exploded.

The size of the explosion was much larger than Hull had anticipated. A golden-tinged fireball lit up the hallway and immediately shredded the walls and floors around it. The blast obliterated entire sections of the hallway. The shockwave tore into the Vice

President's quarters knocking Jansen, Kira and Jennifer into the wall. Debris slammed Hull to the floor just before a wall of fire roared through the room.

As the explosion faded, only blackened, smoking rubble remained of the Vice President's quarters, the hall outside it, and the quarters on the opposite side of the wall. Alarms began to blare and the station's fire system (what was left of it in the immediate vicinity) activated. Clouds of halon gas sprayed from the roof and smothered all fires in the area. As the asphyxiant began to interact with the atmosphere, it pushed the oxygen away limiting the fire's fuel. It also, unfortunately, limited a basic necessity for the humans remaining in the area: breathable air.

As Jansen lifted himself from the floor amidst the white cloud growing in the room, he coughed hard, unable to catch his breath. Panicking, he lifted Jennifer from the floor and tried to get her above the gas, but it was no use. The gas was suppressing the oxygen. Falling back to his knees, he tried to get up again, but couldn't find the strength. It felt as if he were taking copious amounts of battery acid into his lungs with each breath. Falling forward, he looked up to see soldiers with oxygen tanks strapped to their backs, and masks over their faces charging into the room. The first one stopped and pointed to Jansen, Jennifer and Kira. "Get them out of here now! We don't want them dead!" The guards immediately began to attach oxygen masks to the crew's faces.

"Sir," another guard shouted from the kitchen area. Looking down, he had spotted an arm reaching out from the wreckage. "I found another one!"

"Can you get him out?" the commanding guard asked.

"Yes, sir," the guard said, dropping down. Immediately, he began to pull debris away from Captain Hull. Reaching into the pouch slung over his shoulder, he retrieved a small respirator and attached it to the captain's face.

The lead security guard activated the flashlight on his pulse rifle. Swinging it around, he saw several highly charred papers and destroyed datapads scattered about the floor. Motioning for another guard to join him, he pointed down at the paper and pads. "I want all this gathered up and taken directly to Chief Ramirez's office. This is what we came for."

"Yes, sir," the guard replied.

The lead security officer turned and watched the members of Hull's crew being carried out of the room on small hoverpads. Turning back, he stared at the destruction surrounding him. "The chief isn't going to like this."

***

Julie held Jim's hand tightly as she peered around the edge of the corridor. Inside there were several technicians dressed in white lab coats working busily in front of computer consoles. It would probably be the same thing she would be doing right now if not for being in the wrong place at the wrong time. Running her eyes carefully over each tech, she finally spotted her target.

Glancing back at Jim, she let go of his hand for the first time since escaping. "I see him," she whispered.

Jim cocked his head. “What are you going to do? Why are we at the Med Bay?” He waited for a response. “Julie?”

She waved her hand at him trying to dismiss his concerns. Slowly turning around, she smiled broadly. “Trust me.”

Jim closed his eyes and sighed. “I was afraid you’d say that.”

“Stay here,” she said, taking a step away. “I’ll be right back with our ticket out of here.”

Jim wanted to grab her and pull her back, but in the end, he knew it wouldn’t do any good. That was one of the things he always liked about Julie: her strong will. That wasn’t going to change now. Leaning back against the wall, he lowered his head and tried to look as inconspicuous as possible. This was a well- traveled area of the station and security forces were sure to make their way by.

Standing straight, Julie walked into the Med Bay as if she were supposed to be there. Carefully avoiding eye contact with anyone who should glance her way, she stopped and scouted her target again. She found him standing near the back of the bay, hunched over a computer. Grabbing an empty hypo spray from an examining table, she made her way quickly across the gleaming white floors. Leaping forward, she wrapped her arm around the man’s neck and jabbed the injector needle into the side of his neck. Quickly spinning, she put his body between her and the other technicians.

“Hello, Quentin.”

Quentin grunted as the needle dug into his flesh. “Julie? Julie, what the hell are you doing?”

“Getting off this moon,” she growled, “and you’re my ticket. I couldn’t find any of the good stuff, so I had to fill this hypo with floor polish. I imagine that can't be very good for the human body." She pressed the empty injector harder into his neck. "Tell your staff to back off."

"Stay back," Quentin said nervously. "Please, do what she says."

"Let's go," she ordered.

"You're not going to make it off the station, Julie. Think about what you're doing," Quentin pleaded. "I'm your friend, remember? We can work something out."

"That's what you said last time," Julie pushed the needle again. "Then those black armored goons showed up, locked us in the bowels of the station, and tried to kill us! I don't think I believe you anymore."

"Who tried to kill you?" Quentin asked, genuinely confused. "I thought they were taking you to a secure quarantine station."

"More lies?" They were nearing the door. Although where she would go from there was unknown. She hadn't thought this plan through very well.

"That's what Ramirez told me," Quentin answered honestly. "I don't know anything else. I thought you were being taken care of."

"What did you tell him about us?" Julie pressed.

"That you and Dr. Marcus had a perfect bill of health." He tried not to struggle against the needle in his neck. "That's all, I swear!"

"We'll just have to find out for ourselves," she said ominously. Stepping through the med bay doors, she was met by four security personnel with weapons drawn. One in the back had Jim in shackles with his pulse pistol held to the back of his head. Julie lowered her head and sighed. "Crap."

"Put your hands up," the guards commanded, "and release the doctor." Julie glanced up the corridor in both directions looking for an option out.

He eyes slowly moved back to Jim's. Wide with fear, he was pleading with her to run. She knew if she did, she wouldn't make it three steps before they gunned her down. Pulling the hypo free of Quentin's neck, she dropped it on the floor and raised her hands.

Quentin immediately slapped his open palm to his neck and leapt away. He saw the look of confusion and defeat on her face as the guards advanced on her. "Wait," Quentin shouted, "this woman is mentally ill. We need to get her medical attention right away."

The guards grabbed Julie, spun her around, and slammed her face first into the wall. Grabbing her arms, they pinned them behind her back and quickly shackled her.

"I said this woman needs medical attention," Quentin repeated, stepping closer. "That gives me jurisdiction."

One of the guards turned and sneered. "Please step back, Doctor. We have very specific orders from Station Chief Ramirez. If you do not cooperate, we will be forced to detain you as well." He turned and looked at the other three guards. "Take them to the brig."

Quentin took a step back and watched the security force march away with their new prisoners in tow. Pulling his hand free of his neck, he saw a small daub of blood in the center of his palm. Turning back toward the medical bay, he knew he had to act. Something wasn't right. Keying his wristcomm, he tapped in a secure code and pressed send.

"Deck Manager," a masculine voice responded.

"Mr. Furman," Quentin greeted. "How's that rash?"

"Dr. Kelly," Furman replied quickly with a hint of shock in his voice. "It's fine," he stuttered. "Thank you."

"Mr. Furman, you remember that discretion I promised about the particular source of your condition?" Quentin asked.

"Yes," Furman said slowly. He knew instantly he was in prime blackmailing territory.

"I need to call in a little favor," he paused with a smile on his face. "I need some equipment and a backdoor into the brig."

***

"What are we going to do?"

Chris looked at Cody with worry on his face, "I really don't know." Glancing over at the lifeless form of TC-10, his worry deepened. "Doesn't look like we have much of a choice than to wait right now and see what the captain and Vice President can do."

"That doesn't sound very encouraging." Cody frowned. "Stop talking," the guard commanded, lifting his pulse rifle.

Chris shook his head at the guard and leaned back against the wall. Sliding down to the floor, he crossed his legs and sat quietly. Looking up at Lieutenant Cody, he motioned for her to do the same. It had been just about forty minutes since the inspection started, and the other three guards had yet to return. He wasn't getting a good feeling about this inspection. From little tastes of home, to exotic delicacies that happened to make their way onto the vessel, every ship, no matter what affiliation it held, had some form of contraband on board. It was just a part of being a spacer. Depending on what these guards' definition of "contraband" was, they could be in for a long night. Some inspectors would overlook some of the more common forms of contraband and truly focus on the highly illegal items such as drugs, and weapons, but Chris knew they weren't going to leave any stone unturned. They were bound and determined to find any sign that would lead to an arrest, no matter how insignificant.

Lifting his arm slowly, he accessed his wrist computer. Typing in the ship's security code, he watched his rectangular screen flicker to life. Quickly moving through the ship's systems, he accessed the Tereshkova's security network. Turning on the ship's internal cameras, he cycled through until he found what he was looking for. Two of the security guards seemed to be ransacking Kira's quarters. Flipping sheets off the bed and yanking open dresser drawers, they threw them haphazardly on the floor in a pile. Chris watched one of the security personnel pull a small welding torch from his pocket and burn through the lock on Kira's locker. As the lock fell free, he pulled his sleeve over his hand and placed his hand in the newly created hole. Yanking open the locker, he began to root through the contents. Shaking his head, Chris began to switch through the cameras again until he located the final security guard standing in Jansen's quarters. Chris breathed a heavy sigh, as he knew his science officer's predilection for illegal electronics. As the guard turned slightly, Chris could see a stack of several tracers in his hand along with numerous other electronic devices. With a smile, the guard turned and exited Jansen's quarters. Chris could clearly see him accessing his wristcomm as he made his way out.

Chris turned to Cody with a deep frown. "We're boned." Cody let her head fall back against the wall. "Jansen?"

"Jansen," Chris confirmed.

They heard the security guard's wristcomm chime. Lifting his arm, he tapped the activation button. "This is Sonier."

"Lieutenant, place the crew under arrest. We have located illegal contraband on the ship."

Sonier nodded. "Yes, sir." Clicking off his wristcomm, he lifted his pulse rifle and aimed it directly at Chris and Cody. "On your feet," he commanded.

Chris and Cody floated up from their positions and steadied themselves against the wall.

"Under Interstellar Transit Code 6075.3, I am hereby placing the two of you under arrest," the guard stated. "You have the right to remain silent," the guard recited the well-practiced speech, "anything you say or do can be used against you in a court of law. As this station falls under the laws of Earth Gov, you have the right to seek representation. If you cannot afford to do so, then one will be assigned to you. Do you understand?"

Cody let her head fall forward. "Crap."

Chris nodded. "Agreed." Chris turned to face the guard. "I have a statement."

The guard rolled his eyes, but nonetheless nodded.

"We will not put up with this Gestapo crap," Chris growled. "We will exercise every legal right to nail you and that crooked station chief of yours to the wall."

Moving slowly across the room, the guard dug into his back pocket and produced two sets of handcuffs. "Face the wall," he said as he neared them. As Chris and Cody complied, he lowered his weapon, grabbed their hands, and snapped the metal cuffs into place.

***

Impatiently, it ran its diagnostic program again. To its dismay, it came back with the same exact result: ninety-eight point seven percent complete. There was something within itself not automatically repairing. Still, ninety-eight percent was enough to fulfill its programming. Reaching out over its network, it tried to sense the others one final time. There was nothing to be done if the network was down. There was no way to repair it. Running electrical pulses on the cables buried deep beneath the Europan surface, it still couldn't contact the others. Too much time had passed. Perhaps they had been destroyed, or were in such a bad state of disrepair after countless ages offline, they could not be reactivated. Either way, it felt the numbness of being alone.

A warning alarm began to blare within. Snapping up its sensors once again, it detected a small vessel approaching it from the south. At its current rate of speed, it would arrive in approximately twenty-seven minutes. It detected five of the carbon-based life forms aboard the vessel. It paused for a brief second and thought about reactivating its defense mechanisms, but ultimately decided the vessel and those it ferried were no threat to it. It was nearing its maximum efficiency and would begin work at nearly the same time they would arrive. Once its program had been initiated, there would be no way to stop it internally, or externally.

Keeping an eye on the vessel, it began to shut down nonessential systems. It still hadn't been able to fully repair its memory core, but recovery of large chunks of data had occurred. It would have to be enough. The files containing the exact specifications it needed to operate and complete the task were damaged as well. It had a nearly complete picture, but there were a few small gaps missing. It would have to rely on the automated systems to finish properly. It didn't foresee a problem, but it also knew it was a delicate balance of factors which made a planet habitable.

An idea occurred as it uncovered another missing sector of memory. Activating its sensors, it reached out across the distance to the other major moons in the system. Similar systems were in place on two others in case of a catastrophe. Ignoring the moon closest to the gas giant they orbited—it had never been habitable due to the active volcanoes and proximity to the gas giant's radiation belt—it instead focused its sensors on the third and fourth moons in orbit. Reaching out, it found no trace of life on any of the moons. It seemed to be the only one left active. It knew other moons in other planetary systems had also been fitted with its kind, but its sensors were far too weak to detect them across the vast distance.

Returning to its main task at hand, it saw the last few digits roll over to zero on its diagnostic panel. As it had been preoccupied with finding others of its kind, it hadn't noticed that the automated repair program had finished its task. It was now at one hundred percent operational. It whirred with satisfaction as it moved up its timetable. It could begin the process much sooner now. As it made final preparations, it noticed the vessel drawing closer.

***

Marching across the promenade deck for the second time today, the Vice President was boiling with anger. Walking this well-traveled route, he easily turned around the atrium and headed straight back to the administration section. Not waiting for the double doors to fully slide open, Wyman grabbed them at their sides and pushed them angrily apart. Picking up speed as he moved down the hallway, Wyman was almost at a gallop as he hit the chief's doors. Charging inside, he found the waiting room empty. There was no assistant at the desk, and the doors to Ramirez's office were wide open. Moving inside, Wyman found Ramirez sitting patiently, his hands folded neatly on the desk in front of him.

"I was wondering how long it would take you to get back here," Ramirez said with a smirk. "Please, have a seat."

Wyman ignored the invitation. "What the hell are you doing? You can't go around arresting innocent men and women!" Wyman yelled.

Ramirez made no move to refute the claim. "It has come to my attention," he lifted a minidisk from his desk and handed it to the Vice President, "that a certain video was made of a meeting I attended at Club Io. It seems my true allegiance has been discovered."

"You're a traitor," Wyman growled. "You will be prosecuted under the fullest extent of Earth law." He snapped his fingers and pointed to the chief. "Arrest this man."

Ramirez looked up to the three guards surrounding the Vice President and shook his head. "I don't think so."

Wyman turned to see the guards pulling their pulse pistols and taking aim at him. "What the hell is this, Ramirez?"

"As of just about an hour ago," Ramirez stood and clasped his hands behind his back, "this station was placed under martial law. In about twenty-five minutes, I will be giving a speech that announces our intentions to secede from Earth Gov. This station, and this moon, now officially fall under the jurisdiction of the Voxx."

Wyman looked at the chief in awe. "You have no authority to do this."

"I think I do," Ramirez answered quickly. Moving around his desk, he leaned against the front facing the Vice President. "We will no longer bow down to the hypocrisy of Earth Government. I will not allow the most incredible discovery in history to be taken and covered up. We will take it and reveal it to the entire solar system during the press conference."

"How do you plan to do that?" Wyman asked, insulted by the words spewing from the chief's mouth.

"I already have a team en route to the artifact," Ramirez announced. "They should arrive in no less than twenty minutes. As the conference begins, we will broadcast their findings globally."

"You're starting a galactic civil war," Wyman said honestly. "Is that what you want? Full scale war?"

Ramirez's face darkened as if a shadow passed over it. "It's not a matter of what I want anymore. You and your cohorts back on Earth have given us no choice. We have to do what is right for all humanity."

"Earth Gov will have ships here in two weeks," Wyman promised.

"By that time, the station will already be locked down and the natural ice surrounding the moon will protect us from any orbital bombardment," Ramirez assured.

"How can you be so arrogant?" Wyman asked. "You're signing away the lives of millions by this single action. Earth Gov and the Ministry of Defense will not stop until this station is back in their possession. They will wipe all you insurgents from the solar system."

"Do you think it will be that easy?" Ramirez frowned. He didn't want to be in this position, but circumstances had forced him. "I've already heard from officials in Mars Gov that support our cause. They are ready to back up us up with whatever we need to protect this finding. They've already offered troops and as many vessels as they can spare. Mars Gov ships are already on their way to the station to form a blockade around Europa Prime."

Wyman stumbled back from Ramirez and fell into a chair. Letting his head fall forward, he let out a long breath. He had no idea what to say, or what to do. He wasn't ready for this kind of burden. He was a leader of soldiers, but had never truly been in charge. He had always taken orders from a power higher than himself. His course was unclear. "Do you really want to engulf the solar system in a war that could claim the lives of our citizens? Is that discovery really that important?"

Ramirez nodded. "It belongs to every man, woman and child, not stored away in some research lab on Earth. It's their right to know what we found here."

Wyman took another breath. Looking up at Ramirez, the anger washed away from his body. He stared at the man before him, not as a rival political leader, but as a man. "Do you have any children, Chief?"

Ramirez shook his head.

"I do," Wyman admitted. "Three boys and a beautiful daughter. All four of them followed in their damned father's footsteps and joined the Ministry of Defense. I promised them no special treatment when joining. Everything they accomplished would have to be on their own terms, on their own hard work." Wyman smiled despite the situation. "They've all done very well."

Ramirez shook his head. "I don't see how this applies to anything, nor do I have time for it."

Wyman waved off the chief's concerns. "Please, hear me out."

Ramirez stared at the Vice President for a moment, before nodding for him to continue.

"My oldest boy and my daughter have already been promoted to captain. My two middle boys have chosen to go into more specialized branches of the MOD. They both command specialized marine teams tasked with going in where no other soldier would dare tread." Wyman looked deeply into Ramirez's eyes. "All four of them would be the first shipped off to war. I always knew there would be a time when this might happen, but I guess as a father, I wasn't really prepared for it." Wyman sat forward in his chair. "We need to come to some kind of compromise. Let's work this out. Don't let the solar system be thrown into what could become a long, bloody conflict."

Ramirez was obviously touched by Wyman's heartfelt admission, but he remained stern. "I can't help you, Mr. Vice President. The decision has already been made. The press conference will go on." He looked up to the guards standing behind Wyman. "Please place the Vice President under arrest."

A surge of anger welled up in Wyman as the guards lifted him from his chair and started to handcuff him. "Earth Gov and the Ministry of Defense will not stop until we have eradicated all traitors." He leaned close to Ramirez. "Including you, you son of a bitch."

Ramirez's eyes hardened. "Take him to the briefing room. He's going to be my guest of honor at the press conference."

Without another word, the guards turned and led Wyman from Ramirez's office. Moving back around his desk, the chief sank back into his chair and hit the controls to close and lock his door. Steepling his fingers in front of his face, he turned in his chair and stared out the darkened window behind him onto the mud and silt, and felt his heart sink into his stomach. This wasn't the path he had proposed. His vote to claim the artifact in a bloodless coup had been overridden almost instantly. It seemed his superiors were just looking for an excuse to go to war, and now they had it. It wasn't even about the artifact anymore. It had everything to do with their beliefs. If they couldn't persuade the government of Earth to pull back their exploration missions and mothball the numerous space stations and colonies in the solar system, they would take them by force.

Glancing at the clock on his wristcomm, he slowly stood. He had to prepare for the press conference. He swallowed hard. This would be a day that would live in infamy for centuries to come. He would be the face of the cause that plunged mankind into what could very well be its final war.

CHAPTER THIRTEEN

Hull sat straight up coughing. Grabbing his chest, he tried to force a breath down into his scorched lungs. He remembered the halon gas that filled the Vice President's quarters after he had set the pulse pistol to detonate. Maybe that wasn't such a good idea after all. Finally taking in a deep breath, he listened to his bronchi wheezing as they contracted and expanded. Looking down, he stared at his naked torso wrapped tightly with white bandages. A few dark brown spots—dried blood—littered the bandages and he could feel the dull throb of pain in his back from the debris falling on him. With each cough, his body ached even more. At least he was alive. The realization suddenly snapped his mind back to the three other people that were trapped in the gas with him.

As he tried to steady his breathing, he glanced around his surroundings. He was confined in a small cell, lying on the bottom bunk of a collection of four built directly into the wall. On the far side was a huge transparasteel window with heavy, crisscrossing metal bars embedded within it. He was in the station's brig, at least he could tell that for sure. Standing, he walked with trepidation to the window. Placing a hand on his bruised rib cage, he placed the other on the cool glass and stared out.

Across the way, he could see Kira and Jansen in lone cells and Jennifer lying quietly in another. Kira and Jansen were sitting on the edges of their respective cots staring at the floor, while Jennifer seemed to be rubbing her temples softly with her heavily bandaged hands. Kira had a silver and blue splint around her forearm that blinked quietly as it mended her broken bones. Jensen, however, appeared to be in the best condition of the four. Only a bit of translucent tape covered a small cut on his forehead. Pressing his face to the transparasteel, he tried to look further down the cellblock to see if Cody and Chris had been detained as well. To his dismay, he could only see empty cells in either direction. That didn't mean anything. They could be on his side of the cellblock, or they may have evaded capture altogether. Hull hoped for the latter.

He pounded on the transparasteel with his fist, but it was no use. The cells were thick and soundproof. There was no way to contact the others. He glanced down at his wrists. Both his wristcomm and computer had been taken. That was no big surprise in this situation, but he had hoped they had been sloppy in their search before throwing them in the brig. Moving back from the window, he sat back down in his cot. Looking up, he saw that Kira had noticed him for the first time. Lifting her hand, she waved across the hall to her captain. With a nod, Hull acknowledged her. Kira lifted both her arms and shrugged. Hull understood the signal and nodded again. Lifting three fingers, he pointed to Kira's cell and then to Jansen and Jennifer's. Kira nodded. Holding up two fingers, she tapped the ship patch on her shoulder and pointed to the cell's next to Hull's. He frowned deeply and understood. Cody and Chris were right next to him. Rubbing his hand lightly across his forehead, he took a slow breath and finally mimicked Kira's shrug.

***

Several systems chimed in the massive empty control room. It was ready. It had just received the final confirmation of its repairs and system readiness. Cranking the ancient power generator up slowly, it waited to see if any imbalance could be detected. It couldn't afford a problem at this juncture. As the reactor attained full power, it was ready to begin. Opening the wires to the rest of its form, it allowed the energy to flood through its circuits. It would take less than three minutes to attain full power. As it made final preparations, it couldn't help but feel proud. It was about to realize its creator's wishes.

***

The whirring of motors distracted Hull. Turning, he saw a panel moving in the cell wall. Watching it raise, he saw a video screen appear below it and flicker to life. An image of a podium came into view with the station's logo proudly stamped on it. Behind the podium stood several ferns and a flag Hull didn't recognize. Maroon in color, the center of it was decorated with a picture of a broken Earth. From up through a crack rose the white outline of a hand with a lightning bolt held tightly in its fist. A simple white V hovered over the image of the Earth. Hull surmised this was the flag of the Voxx. He had seen a similar design on the hulls of several pirate vessels that had attacked the Tereshkova earlier in the year.

The static image of the flag and podium pulled back to reveal several people walk up to it. Among them were Chief Ramirez and the Vice President. Three guards maneuvered the Vice President into position slightly off from the podium so he could be seen behind Ramirez. Ramirez, no longer wearing the UESA uniform, was now dressed in a solid black suit and red tie. Hull noticed a silver pin just below the knot in his tie that looked very much like the Voxx symbol.

"Good afternoon," Ramirez greeted, quickly clearing his throat off mic. "This communiqué is being overlaid on every civilian and government channel." He set a stack of papers on the podium in front of him and quickly shuffled through them. Lifting a small glass of water from the table next to the podium, he took a sip and returned it to its position. His actions betrayed his calm exterior, revealing the nervousness he was feeling. "A little over three weeks ago, an amazing discovery was unearthed here on Europa. This 'artifact' as it has been dubbed, could very well prove the existence of an extinct sentient race who once occupied this moon." He paused for effect. The original blurry image of the artifact appeared in an inset over his left shoulder. "An archaeological team is currently en route to the artifact and we will be bringing you live images of this discovery as they happen. I promise you, this is the biggest discovery the human race has ever uncovered." Ramirez looked uncomfortable in front of the camera. Constantly adjusting the knot in his tie as he spoke, he seemed ill at ease with the direction the last few days had taken.

He lifted a hand and pointed over his shoulder. "Behind me, you will recognize Vice President Wyman of Earth Gov. He was sent here to snatch up this discovery and cover it up." The inset picture of the artifact zoomed to fill the entire screen, giving the first good look at the pillar and humanoid face lying half buried in the mud below it. "His orders, taken directly from Earth Gov President Wilson were simple: recover the artifact and return it to Earth for study and evaluation. Nowhere in those orders was he to reveal the existence of the artifact to mankind." The image on the screen snapped back to Ramirez. "That is why this station, along with the artifact, are now under the control of the Voxx, an organization of freedom fighters determined to reveal the truth to the public. Before ships can be dispatched from Earth or Neptune Station, we have already ensured our safety here on Europa. In less than two weeks, warships from the Voxx and Mars Government will be in place to form an impenetrable blockade around Europa Prime. Any attempt to break this blockade, or subvert Voxx authority will result in the use of deadly force."

Hull watched the transmission in awe. He couldn't believe what he was hearing.

"I have just been informed the research team is about to arrive at the artifact." He placed his hand to the small speaker in his ear as a worried look passed over his face. Turning, he placed his hand over the mic and spoke with an assistant quietly. Turning back to the camera finally, he adjusted his suit jacket. "It seems the research team's Deep Research Submersible Vehicle has encountered something spectacular. We're switching to the live feed from the DRSV's external cameras."

The image shifted to that of a mostly black picture. Loose debris and bits of matter could be seen floating in front of the submersible's cameras as the vehicle neared its destination. In the distance, a green light became visible amidst the darkness.

Behind the image, they could hear the muffled voice of Ramirez ordering the crew to zoom in on the strange, eerie light. As the cameras complied, they could clearly make out what looked like a structure backlit by the glow. Tall, magnificent spires and columns reached high into the water around it as the green light intensified. Moving the DRSV in closer, the image became clearer and more defined. The structure, partially covered with mud and decay, began to throb with energy. The green light seemed to intensify all at once and harden as the image began to shudder and stutter with interference.

"There's something happening out here," the sub's commander's voice could be clearly heard through the static. "Power readings from the artifact are off the scale and only seem to be building."

Ramirez felt a twitch above his right eye. His nervous excitement quickly faded to worry. "Pull the DRSV back, Commander," he ordered. "Get back to a safe distance."

"I don't [static]...possible. Controls [static]...non-responsive," the commander's voice replied through the static, growls, and pops. "Power loss...imminent. Systems [static]...ship failing." They were losing the transmission. Only a few clicks and burps of audio could be discerned from the feed.

"Get them back! Get them back!" Ramirez's voice could be heard shouting behind the ever-brightening image of the structure. The green glow of the artifact filled the picture on the monitor. No longer was any darkness visible in the frame, only the sickly green of the artifact. Between the lines of interference and static consuming the image, they could see the green light transition to white as it reached its maximum level of intensity.

A low frequency rumble began to hit the station, vibrating the walls and floors. Hull stood and placed his hands on the transparasteel walls holding him. The vibration seemed to be gaining in strength as the moments ticked by. Stepping back into the center of his cell, he started to get a sinking feeling. Glancing back up at the screen, he watched a shockwave of green-white energy explode from the artifact and race off in all directions. It would only take moments for the wave to reach the station. Another flash of energy and the camera feed on the DRSV was lost. The image shifted quickly back to Ramirez, who seemed to be standing in awe at the images he had just witnessed. Shaking his head, he quickly pushed away from the podium and exited the stage. Snapping his fingers, the guards followed behind with the Vice President in tow. The screen was quickly replaced with a Voxx symbol and then went dark.

As a major tremor shook his cell, the door suddenly began to slide open. Glancing across the hallway, he saw his crewmates' doors opening as well.

Stepping forward, he peered out through the open cell door nervously. Turning to the right, he noticed the cellblock was empty.

Stepping outside, he looked to his crew. "I think we should get the hell out of here."

Kira, Jansen, Cody and Chris nodded in agreement.

"I'll meet you back at the Tereshkova," Hull commanded. "Head straight for Europa Prime and start powering up the engines."

Chris patted his friend on the shoulder with a nod. "It'll be nice and toasty by the time you get there." He turned and started toward the exit.

Kira looked nervously at her captain. "What are you going to do?"

"I need to get the Vice President out of here," Hull said quickly. "Then you're going to need these."

Hull turned to see Quentin standing in the open door of the cellblock. In his hands, he held a black duffel bag.

Hull moved quickly toward the man, but stopped a few steps short. "Who are you?"

"Dr. Quentin Kelly," Quentin said quickly, handing Hull the bag. "Let's just say that I'm one of the few on this station who appears to still be loyal to Earth Gov."

"You did this?" Hull asked, pointing to the cell doors.

"Get your people out of here," Quentin said with a nod. He looked past the Captain to the two people he was truly here for. "Julie, Jim," he said slowly as the two neared him.

Julie stopped next to Hull and faced Quentin. Her face was stern. "Why?" It was the only question she could think of. It seemed to sum up all her pain and confusion quite elegantly. Her emotions were gyrating wildly as she looked at him. She couldn't help but think that a few hours earlier she had a hypospray stuck in his neck.

"I never deceived you," Quentin said slowly. "Everything I told you was the truth."

She tilted her head slightly and looked at her friend. She couldn't decide whether to kiss him or kill him.

"I came down here to rescue you," Quentin continued. Julie took another step forward.

Quentin could see Jim tensing as if readying to react to whatever Julie had in mind. "Listen," he said, holding his ground, "I'm here to help."

Julie leapt at Quentin. Before he had a chance to pull away, she wrapped her arms around his waist and hugged him tightly. "Thank you."

Jim rushed up and patted Quentin on the shoulder. "I knew you weren't the villain of the piece. Had to be a mistake."

"We need to get off the station," Julie said, turning to Hull. "Can you help us?"

Hull nodded. "That's the plan. We just have to tie up some loose ends." He looked at Jennifer. "Can you get them off on the Armstrong?" Jennifer smiled. "You owe me one."

He grabbed his ex-wife and hugged her tightly, careful of her bandaged hands. "Anything," he offered.

She wrapped her arms around Hull and felt comfortable and safe. It was exactly where she wanted to be. "After we get out of this, we need to talk."

Hull pulled back and looked at Jennifer with wide eyes unable to speak. She slowly pulled away from the embrace and took a step toward her three new charges. "Be careful," she said to Hull before turning her attention to the rest of his crew, "all of you." She turned and headed for the exit with Quentin, Julie, and Jim close behind.

Julie stopped and dug her hand into her pocket. "Jim wait." Jim stopped, anxious to stay with the group. "What?"

She held out her hand. "Here." Jim lifted his open palm.

Julie dropped the flattened penny in his hand. "Thank you. It brought me luck.

Jim held the flattened piece of copper in his hand and smiled. "You're welcome."

Julie briefly lingered in the moment but snapped her attention back as another tremor rocked through the station. Turning, she grabbed Jim's hand and headed for the door. "God, I need a cigarette."

"You and me both," Jim added with a laugh.

Hull watched the brig doors slid shut. Turning back to his crew, he quickly thumbed through the bag Quentin provided. He found two black security uniforms and four pulse pistols. Looking up at his crew, he smiled. "Jansen, you're with me. I want the rest of you on the Tereshkova ASAP."

***

"What the hell is going on out there?" Ramirez asked as he charged into the main control room. Another tremor shook the station, nearly toppling the station chief to the ground. Grabbing onto the back of a nearby chair, he managed to keep his balance. Looking back, he saw his guards haul the Vice President into the room with him. He wanted to tell them to take him to the brig with the others, but there was no time. This needed his immediate attention. "What happened to the DRSV?"

The large, rectangular room was staffed full of technicians. Every chair was full, and at least one person stood behind each occupied seat in case of emergency. Six large screens, arranged in a rectangle at the front of the room, monitored every aspect of the station and the surrounding area. The right two screens contained the last images from the DRSV, while the center two contained live shots of the energy wave from the station. The final two screens showed the station with numerous red, circular lines washing over it.

The control room was buzzing with activity, so much so, it was difficult to make out every sentence thrown at Ramirez. He tried to separate the words and shouts, but couldn't manage it. "Deck Manager," Ramirez shouted. "Where is Deck Manager Furman?"

A balding man wearing the dark blue uniform of the UESA appeared from the crowd gathered in front of the massive screens. Glancing around the control room, he tried to spot the person yelling for him. Locking onto Ramirez, he charged up the steps to the main control deck. "Chief Ramirez," he said impatiently.

Ramirez grabbed Furman by the shoulder and maneuvered him as far away from prying ears as he could. "Simon," Ramirez breathed, looking nervously around the room, "what in God's name is happening out there? What happened to the DRSV?"

Simon wasn't good at hiding his emotions. He was merely a tech, not a politician like the chief was. His face became long at the mention of the sub. "We monitored an explosion shortly after the transmission feed was lost," he answered solemnly. "We think we lost them."

"Jesus," Ramirez said under his breath. His and his superior's majestic plan was going to hell before it even had a chance to get off the ground. “And the status of the artifact?”

“Many of the station’s sensor arrays have been damaged by the intense electrical interference,” he prefaced his answer. “But from what we can tell, the artifact isn’t merely a single pillar as we had originally surmised. It seems to be,” he looked back at the main viewer and the ominous green-white light growing in intensity by the second, “huge.”

“But what is it doing?” Ramirez urged.

“We have no idea,” Deck Manager Furman reported. “The station is taking a beating, though. Electromagnetic shields are down to forty percent. We can’t take much more of this. The artifact is not only generating severe electrical disturbances, but incredible tidal forces as well. It seems to be disturbing the entire moon.”

Ramirez looked from his deck manager back to the Vice President. With a long breath, he turned back to Simon. “Recommendations?”

Another massive tremor rocked the station, spilling techs from their chairs and nearly knocking Ramirez and Simon to the floor. The sound of creaking, bending metal echoed eerily through the station.

Furman looked up nervously at the room. “The hull has been compromised,” he said mostly to himself.

“Mr. Furman,” one of the techs shouted frantically.

Furman turned and charged toward his seat in the forward command. Placing his hand on the back of the tech’s chair, he leaned over and stared at the screens. Taking in the information, he slowly stood and returned his attention to Ramirez. "Pod twenty-three just buckled."

"What?" Ramirez shouted. "What do you mean it just buckled?"

Furman moved across the room and grabbed Ramirez. Pulling him back to the tech's station, he pointed down at the screen displaying a tactical view of the station. "Our outermost pod on the north side, pod twenty-three, just lost pylon support." Furman patted the tech on the shoulder. "Give me a live view."

The tech quickly punched the command into his terminal. He had cycled through four cameras before he found one operational. The static switched to a murky image of wreckage. Through the mud and silt the collapse had produced, they could barely make out that the pod had crumbled to the ocean floor and was pulling pods twenty-two, twenty-one and twenty along with it. Each pod, still connected by bridge tubes, was pointed angrily down toward the ocean floor and threatening to topple at any moment.

Furman tapped his wristcomm and lifted it to his mouth. "All emergency personnel report to pod nineteen," his voice echoed over the station's loud speakers. "Repeat, all emergency personnel report to pod nineteen. Hold there for further instructions."

Ramirez felt a ball of biting, churning rattlesnakes forming in his stomach. "How many people in those pods?" He held his breath and waited for the response.

Furman reached down and quickly accessed a crew manifest for the pods. "One hundred and fifty-two." He stood and looked at the chief. "At last check."

"Recommendations?" Ramirez asked again, this time, hoping to not be interrupted.

"I honestly don't think the station can take much more of this abuse," Furman replied. "I think we need to seriously consider evacuation."

The acid in Ramirez's stomach doubled. Pressing his balled fist to his gut just below his rib cage, he looked at his deck manger as another tremor rocked the station. Taking a deep breath, he nodded. "Send the evacuation order. Alert Europa Prime that a lot of traffic will be heading their way."

Furman nodded. Turning, he tapped the nearest tech on the shoulder and asked for his chair. Sliding in, he placed his fingers gently over the control panel, poised to enter the command. Resting his fingertips on the keys, he activated the emergency alarms. Instantly, klaxons began to sound across the station. Lifting his wristcomm again, he held it to his mouth. This was the one announcement he hoped he would never have to give. "Attention," his worried voice echoed through the station again, "by order of Station Chief Ramirez, all visitors and personnel are ordered to evacuate the station. This is not a drill. Please make your way to the express elevators for immediate evacuation." Furman slowly lowered his wristcomm. "I'll keep a skeleton staff here to monitor the evacuation," he said to Ramirez. "We'll catch the last lift out of here after everyone's gone."

Another major quake hit the station.

"One more of those and our shields will be gone," Furman confirmed. "We'll be susceptible to Jovian radiation and won't last long."

Ramirez nodded and patted Furman on the shoulder. "Get your men out of here as soon as possible." Turning, he motioned for the guards to bring the Vice President with him. Ramirez quickly made his way out of the control room.

***

It was pleased. The process was operating above peak efficiency. It would only be a short time before the reformation was complete. Activating its sensors again, the artifact watched the core temperature of the moon begin to rise. Soon, this small world would be exactly as its creators had intended.

CHAPTER FOURTEEN

Hull, Jansen and Kira stumbled out of the detention area just as the station shook violently. Trying to keep their footing, their made their way quickly across the joining bridge to pod one. The announcement to evacuate had just been given as they reached the main promenade deck. Standing to the side in their stolen security uniforms, they watched a flood of panicked people charge across the deck intent on being the first up the express. As the first half-filled elevators began to rise away from the station toward Europa Prime, Hull watched the men and women, in both civilian and UESA clothing, bang on the transparasteel tubes with their fists shouting angrily at those who had gone before them. It was an extremely volatile situation ready to explode at any moment. Glancing at a few of the UESA men and women, he saw they had pulse pistols firmly attached to their hips. He wondered how long it would take before they would use their weapons to ensure they were evacuated.

A frantic woman dressed in a white lab coat skidded to a stop in front of Hull and grabbed him by the shirt. "What's happening to the station?" she asked frantically.

"Ma'am," Hull said slowly, taking her hands from his shirt. "Don't panic. All we know is the evacuation order has been given."

"You have to tell me," the woman urged. "I saw that thing on the video feed earlier. I'm not stupid!"

"I know, ma'am," Hull said evenly, trying to calm her. "We don't know what's happening either.

We do know that you need to make your way to the express and get to a ship."

"I can't die down here," tears began to stream down the woman's face. "I have a husband and children waiting back on Mars for me."

Placing his hand on the woman's shoulder, Hull looked deeply into her watery eyes. He had no idea how to comfort her, or how to get out of this situation. The clock was ticking and he needed to find the Vice President. He turned back to Kira with a pleading look.

Kira nodded and stepped forward. Taking the woman by the hand, she smiled softly. "My name is Commander India Kira," she said slowly. "I'm going to make sure you get on the next express."

"Thank you," the woman cried, wrapping her arms around Kira. "Thank God for you."

Hull patted his first officer on the shoulder. "Make sure there's an express for us when we return with the Vice President."

Kira nodded and began to lead the woman toward the undulating mass of people clumped around the elevators. "Be careful," she mouthed as she left.

Hull nodded once. He waited until she disappeared into the crowd before turning back to Jansen. "Any idea where the Vice President would be?"

Jansen took a quick breath. "Last I saw, he was with Chief Ramirez. I don't think he would just throw the Vice President in a cell like a common criminal."

"Right," Hull said. "Ramirez is keeping the Vice President with him." Pulling his pulse pistol from his holster, he clicked off the safety and powered it up to full. Cradling the black weapon in his hand, he took a few tentative steps onto the promenade deck amidst the rushing crowd of people. There was no time to search the entire station. He had to make a guess and hope he was correct. "Where would the chief feel the safest?" A sly grin crossed his face.

"His office," Jansen replied quickly. "Officer thinking." Hull nodded. "Let's go."

Turning toward the administration complex, Hull waded into the crush of people and began to force his way through.

***

Chris and Cody maneuvered through the zero gravity of the docking port toward the Tereshkova's airlock. They had been one of the first up the express to Europa Prime. Smashed into the overfull elevator with a dozen panicking people hadn't improved his mood any. Without so much as a stray glance from the security personnel on guard in the main dock, the two had easily slipped through with the rush of people as they headed for their ship. Hovering up, they came around the final corner.

Grabbing onto a support pylon in the corridor, Chris stopped himself. "Frag!"

Cody directed her eyes to the airlock door and saw the subject of Chris' anger. "They locked us out of our own ship," she breathed, allowing a small amount of panic to creep into her voice.

A large, circular lock had been placed directly on the center of the airlock door. The lock magnetically sealed it, shutting down all controls and functions. A keypad was in the center of the lock, a red glow around it.

Moving up to it, Chris began trying different combination sequences on it. As each one was met with a double error beep, he became angrier. "If I ever see that weasel Ramirez again, I'm gonna stomp a shit-hole in him," Chris promised.

Grabbing Chris by the shoulder, Cody pulled him back from the door. Drawing the pulse pistol from her holster, she cranked the weapon up to full power and leveled it at the lock.

"I don't think that's such a good idea," Chris tried to protest. He lifted his arms to cover his face.

It was too late. Pulling the trigger, Cody discharged a bolt of plasma into the lock. As it hit, the lock erupted in a shower of sparks and burning metal. As the smoke began to clear from the docking port, the two watched the lock lurch and fall away from the door. Pushing himself through the zero gravity, Chris hit the controls next to the airlock with the meaty part of his palm. The door whined for a moment, but finally opened. The second door inside the Tereshkova's airlock started to roll open after a moment.

Inside, Chris spotted TC-10 still clingingly lifelessly to the wall. Pushing off, he floated quickly inside and placed his hands on the cool frame of the bot. He turned back to Cody. "Start raising the computers on the bridge. I have a feeling we're going to need to get out of here in a hurry."

Cody nodded and started out of the airlock toward the bridge. "Lieutenant," Chris called after her, a thought occurring to him.

Cody stuck her head back into the airlock. "Yeah, Chief?"

"Make preparations for extra weight on the ship," Chris said slowly. "Why?"

Chris turned and pointed out the airlock. A mass of people was beginning to form just beyond the door. "I think we're going to have a few extra passengers."

Cody smiled. "I'm on it."

Chris began to wave the people into the Tereshkova's airlock. "Come on, people. Let's make this orderly."

As they moved passed him into the main section of the ship, Chris returned his attention to TC. Flipping open the panel on his chest again, Chris nervously began to key in his security code. He hadn't been lying to the security guard earlier. There was no guarantee he could turn TC back on. There was no response from the panel. Not a single light turned on. Nervous energy turned to worry. Slamming his fist against the big bot's chest, he keyed in the security code again. Still nothing.

"Come on, you old bucket of bolts," he pleaded.

Moving back slightly, Chris moved his hands up to the top of TC's chest panel and found the two small latches on either side of his shoulders. Popping them with his thumbs, he wrapped his fingers around the edge of the panel and began to carefully pull it open. Amidst the wires and circuitry, he focused on TC's central computer core. Wrapping his fingers around the central coil that was TC's operating system, he twisted it gently and unlocked it from its position. Staring at the circular component, he tried to see if anything was damaged. He noticed several large scorch marks along the bottom of the white and silver tube.

“Dammit, TC,” Chris grumbled. “You tried to restart yourself after the shutdown, didn’t you?” Placing the damaged core in his pocket, he reached up and grabbed the bot’s head and shook it. “Why did you do that?”

He stared at the husk that was TC. He realized after shutting him down earlier, TC had saved a small amount of energy in his computer core and tried to restart his programming internally. He was trying to be a hero, and had inadvertently blown his safety circuits. Once a TC bot was shut down and locked, physical fuses in their chest prevented exactly what TC had tried to do. Chris wondered what TC was thinking during the shutdown. He obviously knew the fuses were in place, but his overriding need to help his crewmates had forced him to try anyway. It was probable he could be repaired, Chris knew, but TC would never be the same bot again. The computer core contained not only his operating system, but also his brain, personality and every experience that made TC who he was.

Chris reached up and tapped the bot on the head. “I promised I wouldn’t let you die,” he said slowly, “and I won’t.” Closing his chest panel, he moved around TC and floated into the interior of the ship. He needed to get to engineering and start heating up the engines.

***

Ramirez sat in his office with the lights off. Turned away from the desk, he stared pensively out the windows as the green-white light quickly intensified. Swiveling in his chair, he stared at the computer monitor in front of him. Frantic posts from security guards and emergency crews kept appearing on his screen as they tried to get people away from the station. Reports were streaming in from the outer pods of connection bridges being severed with people still trapped inside them. Activating the console in his desk, he quickly cleared the monitor and brought up the station's security protocols. Tapping in his security code slowly so as to not miss a single letter, dash or number, he waited for the system to recognize it. As new information appeared, he lifted his hand and tapped the emergency tab. As it rolled over, he instituted a general distress call. His hopes were low that any ships were near enough to help with the evacuation, but he could try. He assumed it would be far too late by the time the first transport or rescue vehicle arrived.

"So," the Vice President said from the couch on the far side of the room, "planning to go down with the sinking ship?"

Ramirez turned and looked at the Vice President with disdain. "None of this would have happened if you hadn't show up," he growled.

Another quake rocked the station. Ramirez knew another pod had collapsed.

The three security guards standing around the Vice President looked nervously at each other, then back to the Chief. They had no intention of going down with the station, no matter what Ramirez thought. "Chief," one of the guards said slowly, "I think it's best if we get you to the express. If we wait too long—"

Ramirez dismissed the guard's worries. "You men are dismissed. Leave me one of your pulse pistols and get to the express."

The three guards looked at each other with raised spirits. As they moved to the door, one unholstered his weapon and dropped it on the desk in front of the chief. Without a second thought, they slid through the darkened doors and headed for the promenade deck.

Sliding the weapon into his hand, Ramirez leaned back in his office chair. Snapping off the safety, he looked at the Vice President through the eerie glow of the green light filtering in through his windows. "What should I do with you? If I kill you right now, I will be a hero to the Voxx. If I let you go," he said, waving the pistol next to his head as he thought, "I will be branded a traitor and more than likely, executed."

"I vote for the second," the Vice President sneered. "I would make it my sole mission in life to revive the death penalty just to watch you fry."

"That's a lovely thought," Ramirez said with a crooked smile.

The Vice President shot up from the couch and started toward Ramirez. Ramirez quickly leveled the gun at him and shook his head. "Sit down, Mr. Vice President, or I'll blow a hole in you so big, you could put your head through it."

The Vice President begrudgingly sank back down into his seat. "Traitor," Wyman hissed.

"None of that really seems to matter anymore," the chief said with a smirk, "does it?"

"You've already been labeled," Wyman corrected, "by your little broadcast. Earth Gov has, no doubt, already added your name to the 'most wanted terrorists list'. The only way you will ever be safe is if you die down here."

"Don't you think that thought has crossed my mind?" Ramirez asked angrily as he shot up from his desk. Rushing around to the front, he placed the barrel of the gun hard in the Vice President's temple. "Just because I believe a certain way, that labels me a terrorist?"

"How can you be this way?" Wyman asked slowly, ignoring the cold piece of steel digging into his head. "You of all people, how could you align yourself with the Voxx? It must've taken so much hard work to reach this position, the chief of the busiest station in the solar system. How could you throw that all away?"

Ramirez let the weapon drop from the Vice President's head. Taking a step back, he grabbed one of his guest chairs and spun it around. Sinking down into the chair, he stared at Wyman. "I am not John Ramirez," the man said after a moment. "I assumed his identity almost five months ago." The man reached up and touched his face with his fingertips. "The Voxx assassinated Ramirez and through genetic reconstruction and manipulation, planted me in his place."

"My God," Wyman breathed. The ramifications of the statement were staggering. "You're a clone."

Ramirez nodded.

"That's how you convinced Mars Gov to send ships to your aid. Key politicians in their government have been replaced, too." Wyman felt the blood drain from his face. "How can this be? The Moscow Accords outlawed all cloning and genetic manipulation after World War III. All the research was either destroyed, or locked away in the most secure of places."

"We found it," Ramirez assured him. "It was no small order to recreate the experiments either. We had to perfect the science and try and erase some of the mistakes you had originally created."

Wyman finally understood his place in the grand scheme of things, and why he hadn't been killed yet. He let his head fall forward into his hands. "You mean to clone me," he looked back up at Ramirez, "don't you?"

"You are the President's new poster boy for the war on terrorism," Ramirez said with a nod. "To have you suddenly side with the Voxx would be a major coup, don't you think?"

"I'll never let you take me alive," Wyman warned.

Ramirez smiled. "That was never the plan, Mr. Vice President."

Lifting the weapon, Ramirez pointed it squarely at the Vice President's chest. Without a moment of hesitation, he squeezed the trigger and fired a single round. The Vice President fell over in a slump, dead.

Standing slowly, Ramirez tossed the weapon onto his desk. Moving across the room, he grabbed the Vice President and hoisted him up on his shoulder. Walking quickly across his office, he stopped in front of the far wall and held up his hand. A panel, sensing the chief's unique body signature, flipped open in the wall. Tapping a series of controls, a small, round hatch opened. Sliding inside with Wyman's body, Ramirez snapped the hatch closed from the other side. Glancing through the nearly cylindrical space in front of him, Ramirez quickly placed Wyman's body upon a single bed recessed into the wall. Pulling the sheets over the corpse, he moved to the front and slid into a chair directly in front of a single bank of angled windows. Grabbing the control pad, he slid it back and locked it into place in front of him. Working his fingers over the controls, the small escape pod around him began to light up and whir with electricity. Plotting a course for a small break in the Europan ice, he activated the pod's launch sequence.

***

Hull and Jansen charged up through the administration corridor until they spotted Ramirez's office at the end. Stopping just outside the main doors, each drew their pulse pistols. Holding up his fist, Hull opened his five fingers and began to slowly count down. As he reached one, Jansen short-circuited the double doors sending them flying open with a shower of sparks. Rushing inside, Hull swept his pistol over the room only to find it empty. Moving through the open door on the far side of the room, the two men became awash in green-white light. Glancing over the darkened room, they found no trace of Ramirez, or the Vice President.

"Look around," Hull ordered.

Jansen moved to the back of the office and stared out the huge windows at the ever-growing light. It seemed to captivate and frighten him at the same time. He thought for a brief moment that if everything had gone as Hull and the Vice President had planned, he would have been on the DRSV that headed into that mess. Quickly thanking the powers that be for small miracles, he pulled himself away from the window and spun to look at Ramirez's desk. "Captain."

Hull turned to see Jansen holding a second pulse pistol by the trigger guard.

"It was on Ramirez's desk." Clicking the safety with his thumb, he flipped it over in his hand and stared at the digital readout. "It lists a single shot fired."

Hull nodded. Turning back, he worked over the office looking for any clue of the Chief or Vice President's whereabouts. Sweeping over the floor, his eye caught something glistening on the couch. Moving in, he dropped down to his knees in front of it and carefully looked over it. Amidst the dark fabric, he could see a moist spot. Running two fingers through it, he slowly raised them to see two dark spots. Wiping it off on the cushion, he stood and turned back to Jansen. "I think I know where that one shot went."

Jansen looked up curiously.

Hull pointed down to the couch. "Blood. Somebody took a shot right here."

"But who was it?" Jansen asked. "You don't think it was the Vice President, do you?"

"No way to tell without DNA analysis," Hull replied, "and I don't think Chief Ramirez has a spare analyzer laying around his office."

"Captain," Jansen said, returning his attention to the chief's desk, "Come take a look at this."

Hull walked quickly around the desk as another minor tremor ran through the station. "What am I looking at?"

Jansen pointed to the monitor. "Ramirez was here, and he input his security code. We have access to everything in the station's mainframe, including his personal files."

Hull nodded. "Download as much as you can."

"I'm on it." Jansen lifted a blank minidisk from Ramirez's top desk drawer. Sliding it into the console on the desk, he quickly began to transfer most of Ramirez's personal files onto it.

"Skipper?"

Hull lifted his wristcomm and activated it. "Go ahead, Chris."

"Engines are heated up," the engineer confirmed. "Lieutenant Cody has already plotted a course out of the system. We're just waiting on the three of you."

"We haven't located the Vice President," Hull frowned. "We can't leave until—"

A bright orange flash of light outside the chief's windows interrupted the conversation. Running toward the transparasteel, Hull watched a small escape pod blast away from the station and disappear into the darkness. "It was him," he shouted. "He was here the whole friggin' time!" Hull slammed his fist against the window.

"We didn't know," Jansen soothed. "There wasn't anything we could do."

"We let him get away," Hull said through gritted teeth. "I'll bet you that he has the Vice President aboard that pod as well."

Jansen nodded. "I'd say that's a pretty safe bet."

"Captain? Captain Hull, this is Chris. Do you copy?"

Hull looked up into the darkness where the pod had been. It was already long gone. He slowly tapped his wristcomm again. "Go ahead, Chris."

"Lost you there for a second, Skipper. Everything all right?"

Hull turned to Jansen with a nervous look on his face. Placing his head against the window, he moved his wristcomm closer to his mouth. "We lost the Vice President."

Silence.

"Then I suggest you get your ass back here, Skipper. We have about four hundred people who are anxious to get away from this station."

Hull furrowed his brow. "Four hundred?"

"We've taken on a few passengers."

"We're on our way," Hull confirmed. Snapping off the wristcomm, he slammed his fist against the window one last time. "Let's get the hell out of here. Are you finished with the download?"

Jansen lifted three disks and handed them to Hull. "Got as much as I could. I have no idea what's on these disks. I just dragged and dropped."

"Could be a list of every Voxx terrorist," Hull said optimistically. "Could be his grocery list," Jansen countered.

Hull nodded. Turning, the two headed out of Ramirez's office and back to the promenade deck.

CHAPTER FIFTEEN

Curious, it thought. It seemed the carbon-based life forms were fleeing. Raising its sensors, it watched thousands being conveyed away from the surface by some means the artifact wasn't familiar with. This was an odd development. It had no intention of harming this new life form, just preparing this world for the creators. Could it be that the reformation process was actually harmful to these beings?

Activating two of its tractor beams, it locked onto the small vessel that had been approaching before the energy wave had forced it down. Using the beams like arms, the artifact pulled the vessel in close and focused all its remaining sensors on it. It detected a startling anomaly. These life forms were not aquatic like the creators had been. There were three of the life forms still alive in the vessel, while two others had expired. Examining the craft, it learned the life forms were rather fragile, and needed oxygen in a gaseous state to breathe. Their respiratory systems were nothing like the creator's, unable to pull oxygen from the water. Placing the vessel down, it sensed two more of the life forms had just expired. Moving quickly, it created an oxygen environment deep within itself and placed the vessel inside. Ripping open the top with its beams, it allowed the remaining life form to breathe. It sensed the being was moving toward the hatch.

Regret washed over its programming. It was killing these beings by accident. Focusing its sensors to the south, it looked again at an artificial structure it had previously ignored. It seemed to be very much like the vessel, filled with a gaseous oxygen environment. The reformation had damaged this structure as well. There was nothing it could do now though. The process had begun and there was no way to shut it down. Without its partner machines, there was no way to protect this structure either. It had to continue with the process.

Looking beyond the icy surface that covered its home, the artifact sensed many thousands more were being carried away in similar vehicles to the one it had studied. At least the life forms would survive. It would not be the cause of their extinction. It couldn't help but wonder if it was doing the right thing. There was no trace remaining on this now barren world of the creators. Was it destroying an environment in favor of an old matrix, when a new species had just taken a foothold here?

Its programming pondered the question for a moment, but ultimately decided there was nothing to be done. The process would continue, no matter the consequences to this new life form. Turning its sensors within again, it found the carbon-based life form standing outside its vessel. At least it could learn more from this specimen. Reaching the beams within again, it grabbed the life form gently and began to study it. It would have to come to some kind of compromise. At least that was allowed by its programming.

***

The double doors of the administration complex opened wide as Hull and Jansen moved toward them. Stepping out onto the promenade deck, they saw most of the people had already been evacuated. Only a small crowd stood at the base of the express waiting for their turn. Taking a step ahead, Hull heard an uncomfortable splash. Glancing down at his feet, he saw water rushing into the station from a nearby hatch. As another tremor shook the station, he felt the main pod lurch to the left. He realized the support pylons were giving way beneath it. There wasn't much time. They had to get the last remaining people out before the main pod buckled or the express would be useless.

Moving rapidly across the deck, Hull hit the stairs at the back in a dead run with Jansen in tow. Coming around the corner, he jogged to a stop in front of the express. A loud cracking sound behind him caught his attention. Snapping his head around, he watched one of the tallest trees in the atrium sway forward and fall. The mighty oak crashed through the upper deck of the promenade and fell to the floor amidst a hail of debris. A power cable snapped loose from its mounting and was easily sheered in two leaving the lights around them flickering. Glancing back toward the administration complex, Hull watched the water rise further into the station.

Turning, he spotted Kira placing the last of the refugees in two of the twelve tubes. Lifting her wristcomm, she signaled to the express master that another lift was ready to go. Hull saw the woman in the white lab coat in the lift. Turning, she spotted him as well and waved. As the lift began to rise, relief washed over her face. Hull lifted his hand until she disappeared beyond the roof of the pod.

Holstering his pistol, he moved toward Kira and placed his hand on her shoulder. "You stayed here and helped all these people?"

Kira spun and saw her captain. With a relieved smile completely out of character, she placed her hand gently on his face. "I had to wait for you, Captain," she replied. Glancing over the Hull's shoulder, she nodded at Jansen. "Good to see you too, Ensign."

Jansen smiled.

"Let's get back to the Tereshkova," Hull instructed them. "I don't think this pod is going to last much longer."

Kira pointed toward the final available pod. As the three stepped inside, she tapped the access panel hurriedly and closed the door. Activating her wristcomm, she lifted it to her mouth, "Control, this is Europa Station. We have one final express to bring up."

"Acknowledged, Europa Station," a frazzled voice replied. "Be advised current stress sensors on the express are well above dangerous levels."

"What are you trying to say?" Kira asked quickly.

There was a long pause. "I can't guarantee you'll make it before we experience catastrophic failure."

Kira nervously looked to Hull and Jansen.

Hull situated himself in the center of the express and grabbed onto the handrails. "No choice."

Kira nodded. "Understood, control. Bring the lift up anyway." They felt the express lurch once and quickly start to rise the two kilometers to Europa Prime. Glancing back one final time into the station, Hull watched water overtake the first deck of the promenade. They weren't going to make it. The main pod wasn't going to last the ten minutes it would take to get to the docking station. As the express rose past the hull of the station, the glowing green-white light from the artifact assaulted them. Where once they had only seen darkness, they could see for miles in every direction. Mountains, valleys and plateaus all became visible on the Europan surface as the green light washed over them. They could see concentric circles rippling out from the artifact in all directions and disappearing off into the distance. As another of the ripples hit the station, they saw two more pods collapse near the edge of the station. Looking up, he saw a large, white jagged mass sink down quickly from the surface and slam into the ocean floor near the station.

As the express sped toward the surface, Hull was surprised to see clear water above them instead of ice. Passing through its surface, they looked down to see the ice crust of the planet breaking up. Large chunks of ice snapped away from the main sheet and disappeared into the ocean depths. The artifact was warming the planet, Hull surmised. As the express rose further into space, he looked down on the surface of Europa, which was now awash with green light. The very moon was luminous in the blackness of space as it was transformed. He could see large, gaping holes in the ice where the ocean beneath was clearly visible.

Glancing to his right, he saw several small maintenance pods from Europa Prime busily cutting on the tubes. Large pieces of metal had been maneuvered into place next to them. They meant to sever the express, saving Europa Prime.

If the station below were to buckle with the express still attached, it could mean disaster for the docking station. He felt the tube shudder. Looking back down at the moon, he could see the tube beginning to bend.

"Lift ten, this is control. Are you still with us?"

Kira activated her wristcomm. "Still here, control. What's our status?"

"Europa Station just bought the farm," control confirmed. "We're activating our thrusters to try and straighten the tube. You're currently eight minutes out." The express master paused. "We're doing all we can."

"Thanks, control," Kira said, snapping off her wristcomm. She turned to face Hull. "We're not gonna make it, are we?"

Hull's face remained stern. He slowly shook his head.

Kira fell back against the wall of the express and lifted her head. Taking a long, slow breath, she tried to quell the pain and fear running rampant through her system. Above her, she could see the bottom of Europa Prime, and just barely make out one ship in the dock above it. "There's the Tereshkova," she said with a half-hearted smile. She raised her hand toward the top of the elevator. "It's almost like you can touch it from here."

"They're cutting the other tubes," Jansen said, staring down at the moon. "The other lift must've made it."

"No," Kira said, "I can still see them above us. They're only a minute or so ahead of us."

Hull looked up and confirmed Kira's sighting. In lift nine; he could see the bottom of the express elevator. "Control," he said, activating his wristcomm quickly. "Don't cut the tubes! There is still a pod in lift nine! Repeat, there are still people in lift nine!"

"Acknowledged, lift ten," control replied. "We're running out of time. Stress levels are–"

It was then the tubes buckled and broke.

The force of the break knocked the three crewmates to the bottom of the lift. The loud whistle of air escaping the tube became deafening as the atmosphere was sucked away. Grabbing onto the handrail, Hull pulled himself to the edge of the lift as he tried to catch his breath. Glancing down, he could see the tube had broken about halfway above the moon's surface in several places. Large sections of it tumbled through space, now endlessly adrift. There were several of the small maintenance pods quickly rushing to the break with their metal seals in tow. Rolling onto his back, he looked over at Kira and then to Jansen. A large gash was bleeding profusely on Kira's forehead and she looked unconscious. Jansen had propped himself against the edge of the express and was trying to take small, shallow breaths.

Lifting to his knees, Hull slammed his hand against the control panel on the lift's wall. Activating emergency measures, the express was completely sealed off from the tube. They were only left with the air inside the cylindrical elevator, but it was better than asphyxiating as the oxygen was quickly sucked out of the tube into space. Crawling across the floor, Hull grabbed Kira and lifted her torso into his lap. Unbuttoning the snaps on his sleeve, he pushed the cuff past his hand and pressed it to the wound on her head. Applying pressure, he tried to stop the bleeding. Pointing up, he directed Jansen's attention toward the transparent ceiling. As the two looked up, they could clearly make out the details in Europa Prime's hull. They were almost there.

Painted in bright red lettering, Hull saw the latest addition to the station. "Thank you for visiting Europa." Letting his head fall back against the wall, he allowed himself a brief laugh.

As the express rose the last few meters into Europa Prime, Hull saw several technicians racing across the floor toward them. Arriving at lift nine first, they began slicing through the tube until a hole had been created. Pulling the passengers out, they replaced the piece of transparasteel they had just removed and welded it back into place. As the docking clamps grabbed Hull's lift, he watched the techs repeat the process on his tube. As the hole was cut, they quickly set the section aside and began to lift Kira from the express. Tapping Jansen on the shoulder, Hull made sure he was the next out. Following closely behind the ensign, he crawled out of the lift just as the techs placed the chunk of metal back into place. Sparks erupted from the welds as they sealed the tube.

Falling onto the floor of Europa Prime, Hull took a deep breath. Glancing down through the transparent floor, he saw Europa was now a glowing green ball of energy. It pulsed and rippled as the waves of energy washed over and back into each other. It was beautiful.

CHAPTER SIXTEEN

Slowly, Captain Hull slid back into the captain's chair on the bridge of the Tereshkova. Placing his hands on the armrests, he looked out over the familiar setting. The view screen at the front was completely dark, and only a few sparse lights from the stations illuminated the darkened bridge. Leaning his head back for a moment, he took a deep breath of the recycled air and relaxed. Closing his eyes, he took in the familiar smells of computer terminals and grease from the pneumatic door behind him. Running his thumb over the controls on his chair, he jabbed two keys and activated the screen. Rotating the cameras on the Tereshkova, he stared down at the ball of glowing light that was Europa. It seemed to have dulled slightly, but not enough to take away from its beauty. It glowed like an emerald in space, hovering just above the red, orange and yellow bands of Jupiter's atmosphere.

He heard the door behind him hiss open. Turning, he watched the four members of his command crew filter onto the bridge. Without a word, each slowly climbed into their stations and began to activate them. An air of regret hovered in the air as they worked. Hull had only moments before told them of Ramirez's escape and the Vice President's loss. It wasn't their fault, he knew, but he felt responsible. He and his crew had been charged with ferrying the Vice President to Europa and bringing him home when his mission was complete. In that sense, they had failed. He took another breath and tried to clear his head. Earth Gov had already been informed, and there was nothing to do but head home now.

He turned to his left and glanced down at Ensign Jansen. "Science?"

"Acknowledged, and on-line," Jansen said quickly.

Hull nodded. This marked the beginning of their third week together, and he couldn't think of anyone he would rather have sitting beside him. Jansen had shown true courage in the face of danger, and as far as Hull was concerned, was a member of the family now. Turning away from the young ensign, he directed his attention to his oldest friend on the bridge. "Engineering?"

"Acknowledged," Chris replied quietly, "and on-line."

Hull knew he was still reeling from the loss of TC-10. There was nothing he could say or do to ease that pain. If he brought it up, Chris would just brush it off with his traditional macho brogue. He needed to let his friend grieve. Turning forward, he looked at the two front seats. "Tactical?"

"Acknowledged," Kira said, peering over her chair. A large white gauze pad was bandaged to her head to cover the wound. Small specks of dried blood were visible beneath it. "And on-line," she confirmed.

Hull looked to the final station on the bridge. "Navigation?"

"Acknowledged," Cody replied, "and on-line. Departure course has already been plotted, Captain."

Hull smiled at the eagerness of his helmsman to leave the system. He was also proud of her. He had seen her develop from mousy into a rather extraordinary woman in the short time span of their mission on Europa. He tapped another key on his control pad. "Control, this is Tereshkova," he said proudly. "We're ready to depart."

"Acknowledged," Control replied coolly. "You have permission to depart."

"Clear all moorings," Hull instructed.

"You're free to maneuver, Tereshkova," control responded after a moment. "Have a good trip home."

Hull terminated the transmission and looked back over his bridge. "I wouldn't have it any other way. Two," he acknowledged Cody's station, "take us home."

Cody couldn't help but smile broadly. "With pleasure."

"Captain," Jansen said slowly, "we have an incoming transmission."

"From whom?"

"Computers identify source as the UESA Armstrong," Jansen answered. "Put her through," Hull said knowingly. The image of Europa on the main viewer was suddenly replaced with Jennifer's visage amidst a panoramic view of the Armstrong's bridge. Hull stared for a moment. It was roughly semi-circular with Jennifer located in the center of it. The stations were arranged along the back of the bridge with the navigation and tactical stations in front of her. It seemed much brighter and warmer than the bridge of the Tereshkova, but Hull knew that was only due to the color palette chosen and the additional lights installed around the ceiling. He had only toured a Triumph class vessel once, but it had been enough to impress him. He suddenly felt a bit cramped in his chair.

"Captain Hull," Jennifer greeted him. "Good to see that you made it."

"Likewise, Captain," Hull replied. He sat in his chair for a moment just staring at her face. "Where are you headed?"

"To Neptune Station," Jennifer answered. "We've been ordered to pick up several members of the Senate who were touring the station and bring them home to Earth. We have three passengers that are really anxious to get away from Europa."

Hull smiled knowingly. "How are the good doctors?"

"They seem to be doing fine," Jennifer replied. "Julie and Jim have requested a private cabin," she said with a smirk. "I couldn't help but grant their request. Dr. Kelly is assisting my medical staff. There were a lot of people hurt in the exodus." She paused, looking at Alex's face, "Where are you headed?

Hull took a breath and paused. "Home."

Jennifer nodded. "It was good to see you again, Alex."

"You too, Jennifer," Hull breathed. "God speed."

Jennifer stood and smiled broadly at the screen. "Take care, Alex."

Reaching back, she tapped a control on her chair and ended the transmission.

As the screen went dark, Hull was tempted to resume the live image of Europa, but after a moment of thought, he decided to keep it dark on the bridge. It was soothing in some way. "Four," he said slowly.

"Yeah, Skipper?" Chris answered. "Reengage artificial gravity."

"Already on it," Chris replied.

After a moment, the captain felt his body become heavy as gravity was restored to the ship. Giving himself a moment to adjust, he finally stood. Clasping his hands behind his back, he walked slowly over the deck between the sunken command stations.

EPILOGUE

The warship Chicago slowed and eased into orbit around Europa. It's companion ships, the Indianapolis and the Franklin followed suit, remaining in the same wedge formation they had been in ever since leaving Earth. The mighty, black symmetrical hulls nearly vanished against the darkness of space. Only the reflecting light from Jupiter and Europa showed their silhouettes against the stars. Assuming a polar orbit around the small moon, the ships instantly opened their gun ports and began to arm their weapons.

"Europa Prime," a sternly cut man in a black jumpsuit boomed from the captain's chair aboard the Chicago. "This is Captain Hunter of the Earth Gov Warship Chicago, do you read?" He tapped his communication panel again, "Europa Prime, this is the Chicago. Respond."

Static filled the bridge speakers.

Hunter turned and looked over to his science officer. "Are you reading the station?"

The science officer nodded, "I can see the station on my scopes now, Captain. It still seems to have power, it's just not responding to our hails."

Hunter tapped his knuckles on the armrest of his seat. "Theories?"

"There hasn't been any contact with the station for almost two weeks now," science replied. "It could be it's too damaged to respond." Science tapped his fingers over his controls. "Captain, this is incredible."

"What is it, science?"

"Europa is completely free of ice," science responded. "In the span of two weeks, the entire ice shell of the moon has melted and," science paused, rechecking his readings.

"And what, science?" Hunter asked impatiently.

Science looked up at the captain in awe. "There is an oxygen atmosphere forming around the moon."

"That's incredible," Hunter breathed. "What caused this?"

"Captain," the tactical officer shouted from the front of the bridge, cutting off the response from the science officer, "I have three new signals closing in on our position."

Hunter stood and walked toward the front of the bridge. "On screen." The view screen snapped to life. Above the now completely watery moon of Europa, Hunter could see four ships bearing down on them. Their configuration was very much like his ship. "Identification?"

"I'm reading the Cydonia, the Olympus, and the Deimos," tactical replied. "Transponders identify as Mars Gov."

Hunter quickly moved back across the bridge and into his seat. "Weapons?"

"Sensors indicate the warships are hot," tactical answered.

"Captain," science broke in, "we're receiving a signal from the ships. It's a recorded message and seems to be repeating every ten seconds."

"Put it on speakers," Hunter ordered.

"…Violating Voxx space. You have sixty seconds to exit the system or you will be fired on for violating Voxx space. You have—"

"Kill that," Hunter ordered. "Voxx space, my ass," he said under his breath. "Navigation, turn us around." Hunter keyed a command into his console. "Indianapolis, Franklin," he said sternly, "This is the Chicago. We're going to war." Tapping his finger on the console, he looked over his bridge. This is what they had come for, and their orders were very clear. They were to retake Europa at all costs.

"Are we in firing range?" Hunter asked as he stared at the massive, black ships on his view screen.

"Five seconds, Captain," tactical responded.

Counting down the seconds in his mind, Hunter leaned forward eagerly in his chair. Wrapping his hands around the armrests, he squeezed until his knuckles began to turn white. Without blinking, he stared at the ships on the screen. Reaching the final number in his head, he took a quick breath.

"All forward batteries," he gritted his teeth, "Open fire."

By The Author

Fallen Angels
Biogenesis – Fallen Angels Book Two
Crusade – Fallen Angels Book Three
Phantoms (OPR Book One)
The Abydos Triad (OPR Book Two)
Caitlin (OPR Book Three)
Darkness
Exodus: Europa
Until The Stars Grow Cold
Devlin's Hollow
At The End of All Things

www.ingramcontent.com/pod-product-compliance
Lightning Source LLC
LaVergne TN
LVHW030910080826
845145LV00010B/2846

* 9 7 8 1 7 8 6 9 5 5 1 0 4 *